I0613379

Benjamin E, Rich

Mr. Durant of Salt Lake City

Benjamin E, Rich

Mr. Durant of Salt Lake City

ISBN/EAN: 9783337295417

Printed in Europe, USA, Canada, Australia, Japan

Cover: Foto ©Andreas Hilbeck / pixelio.de

More available books at **www.hansebooks.com**

MR. DURANT

— OF —

SALT LAKE CITY,

"THAT MORMON."

BY BEN. E. RICH.

"God attributes to place
No sanctity, if none be thither brought
By men who there frequent."—MILTON.

SALT LAKE CITY :
GEORGE Q. CANNON & SONS CO.,
PRINTERS.
1893.

PREFACE.

MORMONISM is a subject which has been handled by many authors. Some have written in its favor, with prayerful hearts, seeking the guidance of the Holy Spirit as their honest convictions were recorded; while others have declared against the Mormons and the man who was the instrument, in the hands of God, of founding their faith. A few of the latter class have been honest in their attacks, believing, perhaps, that they were doing the Lord's will in opposing it; but the majority have been actuated by hatred in all they have said on the subject.

The author of this work has endeavored to present, in plain and simple words, the faith of the Latter-day Saints, with a desire to aid and interest the young men of Mormondom, who have had no missionary experience, and to fit them to make known their belief to the nations of the earth, should they be called upon for that purpose.

If this book shall benefit them, and give others a better conception of the Latter-day Saints and their religion, the object in publishing it will have been attained.

THE AUTHOR.

OGDEN, February, 1893.

CONTENTS.

CHAPTER V.

FURTHER DISCUSSION OF THE FIRST PRINCIPLES.

CHAPTER VI.

TRUTH AGAIN DEFEATS FALSEHOOD.

CHAPTER VII.

CHAPTER VIII.

THE PROPHET JOSEPH'S STATEMENT.

CONTENTS. vii

CHAPTER XIII.

ABOUT THE MORMONS.

CHAPTER XIV.

MR. BROWN'S LETTER TO THE MARSHALLS.

' CHAPTER XV.

CONCLUSION.

APPENDIX.

WHAT BRIGHAM YOUNG SAID.

MR. DURANT OF SALT LAKE.

CHAPTER I.

THE OLD AND THE NEW.

THERE are few if any cities or towns of any consequence in the vast territory known to poesy as the Sunny South, that do not speak in every street corner, in almost every building, and even through the individuals themselves, of the wondrous changes wrought by the great civil war. Those who knew that Sunny South before the sanguinary struggle, and have since looked upon it, will most readily appreciate the force of this statement ; while those who have not seen it, need only be told that where villages existed then, now thriving towns arise, or bustling municipalities ; elegant mansions have supplanted log huts or other indifferent abodes of men ; the railway has displaced the stage coach for all time ; newspapers abound where

2

before these were almost unknown, and—greatest boon of all—the auction block, whereon human merchandise was publicly vended, exists only as a memory which itself is rapidly vanishing before the pressure of modern progress and a better civilization. In one respect at least, however, there has been little, if any, change, and that is in regard to the best feature of all among the many that are commendable in the true Southerner—the stranger or wayfarer is received with the same unaffected hospitality as of yore, and is at liberty, within reasonable limits, to avail himself of all the conveniences and enjoyments of whatever home he may find himself the guest.

Notwithstanding their hospitality, the people of the South are usually disposed to be suspicious of strangers until well acquainted with them, and they are overly watchful, jealous and even irritable when once a real or fancied cause for vigilance arises. Inheriting traditions and propensities which are inseparable from the

climate and the race, they brook no interference
with their peculiar views, and anything savor-
ing of intolerance or bigotry concerning a
cherished Southernism is summarily suppressed
if it can be ; apart from this, it matters little
what the visitor believes or practices in a general way. In politics they incline largely one
way, possibly for the reason that to do otherwise would, as they look upon it, threaten them
with the domination of the black race, and this
of all things they will not have, no matter by
what means it is prevented. In religion they
are protestant with heavy leaning towards the
Baptist doctrines, not always free from narrow-
ness, yet fairly tolerant—many evincing a willingness to listen, and demanding a right to
believe or disbelieve, as their judgment may
dictate.

Those who are unacquainted with the situa-
tion would be inclined to say at this point,
What a grand field for missionary work ! And
so it is ; but the great mistake of supposing

that the South is deficient in the matter of Christian endeavor or ecclesiastical institutions, must not be made. Far from that! On the contrary, perhaps religious feeling is more generally diffused, guarded, and defended as herein expressed, than in any other section of the civilized world ; but it is not of the kind from which riots and persecutions grow for no other reason than that it is opposed.

There is much else south of the imaginary dividing line of North and South that might be spoken of to interest, but which will not be referred to except incidentally in the succeeding chapters. What we have said is for the purpose of giving only so much of a description of the country and people as is necessary to make our little narrative, the incidents of which are laid there, more easily understood. As this book deals principally with actual occurrences, and people in real life, such a foundation seems to be entirely proper.

CHAPTER II.

A NEW ARRIVAL IN THE TOWN.

A TOWN pleasantly situated in the south-western part of Tennessee, the name of which for the present shall be Westminster, was at the time of which we write one of the most cosmopolitan places imaginable for its size,—that is, for a southern town. It contained probably two thousand regular inhabitants, but these were constantly augmented, it being at times a rallying point for tourists from every clime, and the temporary abode of men who, in the aggregate, during a season, came well-nigh representing every shade of opinion, if not every phase of character.

A quiet little hotel, or perhaps it would be better to say a residence, with accommodations for a limited number of guests, was situated near the outskirts, and so pleasant in all respects

were the location, surroundings and appointments, that its name, Harmony Place, did not
seem at all inappropriate. In two important
respects it was unlike any other hostelry in the
town—there was no bar, and the guests all had
an air of respectability in keeping with the
house itself. It was kept by a planter, in ordi-
nary financial circumstances, whose name was
Marshall ; he was assisted in his duties by a
colored roustabout of uncertain ancestry, a
circumscribed present, and a future wholly
undefined. Mr. Marshall's wife, and daughter
Claire, did their part by generously entertaining
the visitors. · There were at the time of which we
write three guests—a lawyer named Brown, who
had established himself at Westminster; a doctor
calling himself Slocum, who was giving the
town a trial with a view to locating in it if the
patronage warranted ; and a tourist whose
name was given as Reverend Fitzallen, and
whose object seemed to be the pursuit of
health, pleasure and information, and incident-

ally, the dissemination of the gospel according to his faith. Naturally, with so limited a circle of patrons, each having been there for some length of time, the associations all around were more like those in a family than such as exist between landlord and guests. An evening in the parlor with everybody but the Ethiopian present, the daughter singing to her own accompaniment on the piano, while the doctor turned the music for her, was often enjoyed, and there was rarely if ever a discordant circumstance to mar the serenity of these occasions.

It was early in September, 189—, the most enjoyable part of the year in Westminster. A man, who was readily distinguishable from the town-folk, not only by his strange face but by his attire, and by that indescribable air which appears the more plainly the more a stranger tries to discard or conceal it, made his way leisurely to the gate fronting Harmony Place, and continued his way up the walk leading to

the door. He was met by Mrs. Marshall and
informed, in response to his inquiry, that he
could obtain lodgings there. The colored man
took the guest's valise and led the way to a room
on the second floor. After washing himself and
brushing off the dust from his clothes, the
stranger reappeared in the sitting room, and
taking up a paper waited the announcement
that refreshments were ready, which was not
long in coming.

He was somewhat above medium height, well
proportioned, not unusually well dressed, but
still appeared presentable in good society, and
had a countenance which, while not decidedly
handsome, was regular and of that caste which
attracts attention; his voice was quite pleasant,
his natural conversational faculty proved to
be good, and he was so well fortified with
current facts and all the pleasantries of the day,
that before the meal was over he was quite in
harmony with the hostess, who was not only
happy to answer any question he asked, but

took advantage of every opportunity to propound queries for herself. Within an hour
from the time of arrival, the new guest seemed
to be nearly as well acquainted as if he had
been an inmate of the house for a month at
least. This ability of rapidly forming
acquaintance is very rare; and particularly in the
case of travelers, no amount of money or graces
can recompense its absence. Those who
possess it do not need an extended reference to
its usefulness to be made aware thereof, while
those who are not in possession of it can never
be made fully to understand its value by means
of cold type and white paper.

The landlady has learned the name of the
latest arrival before the reader has—it is Charles
Durant, aged thirty, and he comes from the
West—a rather indefinite abiding place to those
of us who are residents of, or are familiar with,
that division of our country. It is satisfactory,
however, to a majority of our eastern and
southern brethren who have never placed feet

upon the shores of the Missouri, or crossed its waters, and who seem to entertain a vague idea that Westerners all come from one place, and are all alike in most respects.

Later in the day Durant took a stroll through the suburbs of the town, and returning was introduced to Mr. Marshall, to the guests, as they appeared one by one, with all of whom he was soon on the most cordial terms, and finally to the young lady, the sole representative on earth of her devoted parents, who, being twenty years of age, as pretty as a dream, well informed, and altogether attractive, was not likely to bear their name much longer, albeit at this time reveling in "maiden meditation, fancy free."

It was truly an interesting circle and the interest did not abate in the least by reason of the latest arrival.

CHAPTER III.

NEW ACQUAINTANCES AND AN AGREEABLE DISCUSSION.

THE evening of the first day that marked the stranger's advent into Westminster saw the entire *personnel* of Harmony Place on the veranda; the new moon smiled benignly upon them, the evening was cool and the "ripe harvest of the new-mown hay" gave to the air a "sweet and wholesome odor." One subject after another was taken up, discussed and disposed of, or at least laid aside to give way to some other, and in each and all of them our hero (for such we may as well commence to recognize him) took a part, and exhibited a fund of information and an aptitude of presentation which gave him the preference without a contest whenever he chose to speak. This became more and more frequent as the night wore on, for there was no disguising the fact that he

was, like the others, already one of the household. If any one of the party wondered what
it was that he had come for, how he expected to
get it, or how long he was to stay, the con-
jecture never found expression; for they all experienced so much of general satisfaction in
hearing him, and took such genuine pleasure
in his word-painting of western scenes and
events, that they were all willing to have him
stay indefinitely. He was literally chosen as
one of their number without opposition, and
the mere matters of detail regarding his
purposes might be left to the future or be entirely undiscovered ; he was now decidedly the
architect of his own fortune so far as retaining
the good will of that little group was concerned.

The conversation proceeded from point to
point until the topics of the quiet gathering
assumed more the aspect of an intellectual
melange than anything else ; the Sepoy re-
bellion made way for the Dakota blizzard, the

signal failure of the first laying of the Atlantic cable was shelved to make place for Webster's artistic destruction of Dr. Parkman, and Cromwell's career of conquests and crimes was followed by a brief discussion of the science and practice of silver mining. (Variety and scope enough, surely!) It must be noticeable that the two subjects which agitate us nationally and sometimes locally more than any others—politics and religion—had so far escaped; they had not, however, been unthought of, and presently the latter was begun by the minister saying:

"Representing to some extent as I do, the church, I am compelled to admit that in the matters of organization, discipline and places of worship, America is thoroughly Christianized. Look at the profusion of church buildings wherever you go. To me such rivalry is gratifying in the extreme, representing as it does the highest type of good citizenship."

"I partially concur with you," said the · lawyer, "and yet I belong to no church at all—

do not, in fact, endorse Christianity as a depart-
ment of civilized life."

"Why, how is this?" said Fitzallen, "I
thought nearly everybody in this country must
be orthodox to some extent at least."

"Not so with me, I assure you," the other replied, "and the strangest part of it is that my
'peculiar views,' as you may call them, are not
the result of neglect or indifference, but are
rather caused by investigation and the peculiar
explanations, or rather lack of explanations, of
those who make the dissemination of religious
views their calling."   .

"In other words you are an unbeliever."

"Exactly."

"Not totally, I trust."

"Oh, not necessarily. The creeds which base,
or profess to base, their tenets upon the Bible
do not, as it appears to me, live up to their pro-
fessions, and the clergy—meaning no offense
whatever—are more addicted to money-getting
than to soul-getting. That there may be

salvation and a Supreme Judge who provides it is to me simply like the traditional Scotch verdict—not proved."

The stranger from the west was listening to all this with the air of one deeply interested. It was as if an opportunity which he desired, but had not expressed himself concerning, had come, and he was not at all reluctant about replying when questioned as to his own views. It came when the churchman, after announcing his determination to "labor" with the infidel, turned to the new-comer and said:

"I do not know whether you would be for or against me in such a work, but coming from what we of the East are prone to regard as the land where restraints are not severe, I fear you might be disposed to assist him rather than me."

"Well, gentlemen," said Durant, "this topic interests me, and while I and my opinions are unknown to you all, still I will, if agreeable, endeavor to throw some light upon the subject

at present, and will seek to do more in that
direction hereafter if favored with an opportunity. I am a believer in religion, laying
claim to a testimony from above, and still I
often find myself opposed by ministers ; they
are generally the very persons who are fore-
most in opposing me on every side, strange
to say."

"I cannot imagine why this should be the
case," said Fitzallen, "if you are as you state,
a true believer in Christ and have a testimony
of Him."

" It may seem strange to you, at which I do
not wonder. But I am afraid I am delaying
the work you have planned for Mr. Brown's wel-
fare. If you will permit me to ask a few
questions during your conversation with him, I
may be able to take a general part in it before
it closes, provided, however, that should we
differ upon any religious views, it will be in a
friendly and pleasant manner."

" Oh, certainly," said the churchman, " I am

sure it will be a pleasure to me to have you join in our conversation as you see fit, and I do not doubt that Mr. Brown and the other gentlemen will look upon it in the same way."

The entire party here expressed approval of the proposed discussion, and the lawyer said :

" I have not the slightest objections, and will be glad to have all the light possible thrown upon the different doctrinal points that I do not believe, and mainly because of which I am not at present a member of any Christian church."

" Then, Mr. Brown," said Fitzallen, "let us commence our voyage in search of eternal truth. What particular part of the Christian faith appears to you as being most difficult to understand"?

" I confess there are many. However, let us commence with one of the principles of your belief. I will refer to some of the literature of the Church of England. The first article of religion contained in the Church of England

3

Prayer Book is: 'There is but one living and
true God, everlasting; without body, parts or
passions; of infinite power, wisdom and goodness; the maker and preserver of all things,
both visible and invisible; and in the unity of
this Godhead there are three persons of one
substance, power and eternity,—the Father, Son
and the Holy Ghost.' According to this, then,
your belief is that the Father, Son and Holy
Ghost are one person, without body, parts or
passions."

"You have certainly quoted correctly from
the prayer book; I fail to see anything wrong
with that. What fault have you to find with it?"

"None whatever if you really believe it, because there does not seem to me much variance
in our conclusions if you believe in such a God
as this ; I can not conceive of a just God who
has neither body, parts nor passions. So far as
the Bible is concerned, I fail to see from what
part of that book you obtain such a conclusion."

" Well, Mr. Brown, using your own language,
'so far as the Bible is concerned,' let us do as
Isaiah commands, go 'to the law and to the
testimony,' (Isaiah viii: 20) and I will soon convince you that the Bible plainly sets forth the
fact that the Father and the Son are one. In
fact, Jesus Himself declares that He and His
Father are one. (John x: 30.) Is this not true?"

" Excuse me," said Durant, "but is it not more
reasonable for us to believe He meant that He
and His Father were united in all things as one
person?—not that they were actually one and
the same identity?"

" Certainly not," said the reverend, "our
Savior meant just what He said when He declared that He and His Father were one."

" I must certainly differ from you," said the
stranger, "for He also asked His Father to make
His disciples one, even as He and the Father
were one, as you will see by reference to John
xvii: 20 and 21, and by your argument it must
have been His wish for those disciples to lose

their separate and distinct identities. I am afraid you are not making a very favorable impression on Mr. Brown's mind."

"Stranger," said Mr. Brown, "your view of the case, I must confess, appears to be very reasonable. Looking at it from any other standpoint would not be in accord with sound reason."

"Let me ask," said the preacher, "did not Jesus say, ' He that hath seen me, hath seen the Father?'" (John xiv: 9.)

"Yes," said the westerner, "for as Paul says, ' He was in the express image of His (Father's) person,' (Heb. i : 3), and this being the case Jesus might well give them to understand that when they had seen one they had seen the other. When Jesus went out to pray, He said, 'O, my Father, if it be possible, let this cup pass from me: nevertheless, not as I will but as Thou wilt.' (Matt. xxvi : 39.) Now then, to whom was our Savior praying? Was He asking a favor of Himself?"

"Oh, no; He was then praying to the Holy Spirit."

"Oh, then by such admission you have separated one of the three from Jesus, for in the beginning you declared that the three were one; and now that we have one of the three separated from the others, let us see if we can separate the other two. In order to do this, I refer you to the account of the martyrdom of Stephen. While being stoned to death he looked up to heaven and saw the glory of God, and that Jesus was standing on the right hand of God. (Acts vii : 55.) Would it not be rather difficult for any person to stand on the right hand of himself ? And in order to prove further that Jesus is a separate person from the Father, we will examine into the account of His baptism. On coming up out of the water, what was it that lighted upon Him in the form of a dove?" (Matt. iii : 16.)

"We are told it was the Spirit of God."

"Exactly! And whose voice was it that spoke

from the heavens, saying, 'This is my beloved
Son, in whom I am well pleased?' (Matt. iii:
17.) Now, mind you, there was Jesus, who had
just been raised from the water, being one
person, the Holy Ghost which descended from
above and rested upon Him in the form of a
dove, making two personages; and does not the
idea strike you very forcibly that the voice
from heaven belonged to a third person? And
then, again, I will draw your attention to—"

The churchman was getting warmed up. Said
he : "These are things which we are not expected to understand; and, my young friend, I
would advise you to drop such foolish ideas,
for—"

"Excuse me. Did you say 'foolish ideas'?
Why, my dear sir, we are told in the Bible that,
'This is life eternal, that they might know thee,
the only true God, and Jesus Christ, whom thou
hast sent.' (John xvii: 3.) Therefore, it should
be our first duty to find out the character and
being of God. You say we are not expected to

understand these things, while the Bible says
these are what we must understand if we desire
eternal life. It also says we can understand the
things of man by the spirit of man, but to
understand the things of God we must have
the Spirit of God; and as you profess to be one
of His servants, you are supposed to be in possession of the necessary Spirit to understand the
true and living God, also Jesus Christ whom He
sent. You say God has no body; did our Savior
have one? If so, then His Father had one, for
I have just proved by the words of Paul that
Christ was in the express image of his person.
(Heb. i : 3.) Jesus appeared in the midst of
His disciples after His resurrection, with a body
of flesh and bones, and called upon His disciples
to satisfy themselves on this point by touching
Him; for, says He, 'a spirit hath not flesh and
bones as ye see me have.' (Luke xxiv : 39.)
Then He called for something to eat and He
did eat (verses 42, 43), and with this body of
flesh and bone He ascended into heaven and

stood, as Stephen says, on the right hand of
God. (Acts vii : 55.) Now, if He has no body,
what became of the one He took away with
Him?"

"This is nonsense! You know that God is a
spirit, and I think we would better not delve
too deeply into matters which we are not permitted to comprehend."

"Pray, listen a while longer, for I have yet
more to say in regard to what you call nonsense,
although if it be such, I must insist that it is
Bible nonsense. You say God is a spirit ; does
that prove He has no body? We are also told
we must worship Him in spirit. Am I to understand from this that we must worship Him
without a body? Have you a spirit? Yes.
Have you also a body? Yes. Were you made
in the image of God, body and spirit? So says
the good old Bible. Man was created in the
image of God. (Gen. i : 26, 27.) Then God
has a body, and, consequently, must have parts.
Moses talked with Him face to face, as one man

talks with another (Ex. xxxiii: 11), and he also
saw His back parts.   He promised (Num. xii.,
8) to speak with Moses mouth to mouth. •We
are told in the fifth chapter of Deuteronomy
that He has a hand and arm.   The Psalm
(cxxxix: 16) tells us He has eyes, and Isaiah
(xxx: 27) says he has lips and a tongue.   John •
describes His head, hair and eyes.   (Rev. i: 14.)
And, as for passions, we are told in the Bible
that He has love, wrath, and is a jealous God.
Are these not parts and passions?   My dear sir,
it would appear that all who believe in the
scriptures must conclude that they are parts
and passions, and that the Creator is a God after
whose likeness we are made."

"Well, I had no idea when I commenced this
conversation with Mr. Brown that I was to find
such an antagonist in yourself.   One would
naturally come to the conclusion that you had
made the Bible a study."

"Thank you, you do me honor.   I confess I
have as a Christian studied the record ; in fact,

at a very early age my parents required me to commit and remember a very important verse in that.good old book. It is found in the fifth chapter of the gospel according to St. John, being the 39th verse, and reads as follows: Search the scriptures, for in them ye think ye have eternal life : and they are they which testify of me."

"That is certainly proper, but I must again warn you against plunging into mysteries which we cannot understand."

"But Peter tells us that 'no prophecy of the scripture is of any private interpretation' (II. Peter i : 20), and these are the things which we should seek for information upon; for lack of explanation by the ministers upon these points is, to a great extent, the cause of many persons being in Mr. Brown's frame of mind today."

"You are scarcely complimentary, and if your assertion be correct, perhaps it would be better for me to withdraw and leave Mr. Brown in your hands."

"I beg your pardon, my dear sir," said Durant, "I meant not to offend, I assure you, and intended only to be in earnest; I will endeavor to be more careful during the rest of the conversation."

The lawyer, who was decidedly impressed at this juncture, dispelled what might have been a painful silence by saying :

" Well, I declare, things have taken a very peculiar turn, I seem to be out of the fight altogether. But I want to say this, I have heard more that appears to be reasonable from you, Mr. Durant, regarding these matters than ever before in my life, and I must also admit that if my early teaching on religious matters had been as reasonable, I almost believe I might have been a Christian."

As it was getting late Mr. Marshall here "put in a word," saying :

"It is now getting quite late and perhaps all would like to retire ; if so, I will conduct you to your rooms."

" No," said Mr. Brown ; "we must not go to bed yet a while. I never was religiously interested before in my life, and I wish to listen to further discussion between these two."

The new-comer was more than willing ; but being somewhat fatigued himself, and realizing that possibly there might be a sense of weariness in some of the others, he deemed it best not to continue for the time being, although asked to do so. He then made a suggestion, which was unanimously agreed to : that the subject be taken up on the following evening in the same place ; and so, with mutual expressions of regard and a kind "good night" all around, the party dispersed for the night.

CHAPTER IV.

GAINING AND LOSING FAVOR.

THE western man had not intended to make a stay at the little home hostelry where he was quartered, and where he had became so thoroughly ingratiated all at once. His mission required a frequent "change of base" and constant action ; but he realized that nothing was occurring which was so greatly at variance with his general purpose as to materially change it, and that, a nucleus for possible future engagements having been established, he might as well remain where he was until called elsewhere. Already he was on the best of terms with all, even with the "colored citizen," and he was disposed to make himself entirely at home, as all hands were willing to have him do.

The time for the adjourned meeting on the

veranda came and not only was a quorum
present, but all of the party were there, besides
two or three neighbors who had learned something of what was taking place. After a few
formalities had been engaged in, the discussion
was opened by Durant suggesting to Fitzallen
that it was a little singular that two men
believing in, and upholding, the same good
book should find anything to dispute about ;
such things did happen, however, and perhaps
it was as well, since by free discussion error was
eradicated and truth made plain.

The preacher then asked a question which
must seem to the reader to have been too long
delayed—"May I ask of what church you are a
member?"

"Certainly," said the westerner ; "but before
answering, will you tell me what church edifice
that is to the east of us?"

"That is the Wesleyan church."

"And the one a short distance below here?"

"That is the Episcopalian."

"What other churches are there in this place?"

"Oh, there are the Baptist, the Catholic chapel, and the quarters of the Salvation Army, so called."

"Is that all?"

"Yes, I believe so, and I think enough, unless we have omitted naming yours."

"You certainly have, for the church of which I am a member you have failed to mention at all."

"Indeed? And what is it?"

"The Church of Jesus Christ, sir. Don't you think it would be well if He also had a church in your midst?"

"Why, my friend, they all belong to Him."

"Is it possible? I certainly have no recollection of hearing you even mention His name in connection with any of them."

"You may not have heard His name, but they are all, yes, even the parading and noise-making Salvation Army, engaged in His service."

"Then why not bear His name ?"

"It is a case in which the name need not be connected with the object, and still the service rendered and the objects aimed at are all for Him, as certainly all who engage in the calling of Christianity believe, and as those who practice in the ministry instruct."

"Let us see how this is. Your church members believe in the Lord Jesus, accept the word of God as an exposition of His principles, as well as a command to them, and the ministers instruct them accordingly. Is that so? "

"It is."

"Then I am to understand that all these churches and communicants uphold and practice baptism by 'immersion as set forth in, and enjoined by, the scriptures."

"No ; that is to say, some do, and some do not."

"What is the probable proportion? "

"Oh, I could not say as to that."

"Do not you and the majority of the others

accept of other forms of baptism and in many cases of none at all?"

"Yes."

"Does not that depart from the teachings of the Bible and the example set by Christ Himself?"

"Not necessarily."

"Did not He go down into the waters of baptism and receive immersion at the hands of John the Baptist?"   .

"Yes."

"And did not the injunction go forth which forms the very corner-stone of His own Church—of Christianity—' Repent and be baptized ?'"

"Yes ; but He did not say that of necessity all were to be immersed. The Bible is fertile in parables and much that is said is left to the intelligence of the reader for interpretation."

"By the same authority I have warned you already against ' private interpretations.' However, we need not rest the case entirely upon

4

that. Take up your Bible at your leisure and examine well all accounts given of cases where this ordinance was performed, and you cannot help admitting that baptism by immersion was the only way in which the ancients accepted that principle. You will see that the word of God *commands*, in unequivocal language, the ordinance of baptism by immersion, and His Son set us the example by going down into the waters. Therefore, those who do not perform this have no claim upon the Savior's name, for they obey not His Father's words nor His own example."

"You would hold, then, that those who do not conform literally to such example are not Christians."

"They may believe in Christian conduct and practice righteousness within a certain sphere ; they may be upright and just in their dealings and their hearts may be filled with love for their race, but they cannot establish rules of conduct for themselves and claim to act in the authority and name of Christ. He has set the pattern and it is for them and for us to follow."

" I never heard such strange reasoning before, and it reminds me of a fact upon which I have often dwelt—that sophistry and logic may both rest upon the same foundation, not, however, accusing you of dealing in sophistry or claiming that in all respects my words have been those of logic. Now, to follow your theme further in the same vein and employing precisely your method of arriving at conclusions—those who do not, for instance, practice the laying on of hands for the healing of the sick, or for the casting out of real or imaginary devils, who do not, for example, subscribe to all the superstitions and resort to the practices enjoined by the Bible—which practices must have had reference to a time in which the domain of science was so limited that it could not even comprehend the present—that all such people, I say, are also outside the pale of Christianity—are pagans, infidels, in fact?"

"You state part of the proposition correctly enough, but your conclusion is unjust—unjust because not a natural outgrowth of the premises stated, and also unjust because containing a reflection."

"I meant no reflection at all."

"So I may readily believe. Now, a man may be entirely outside the pale of practical, or if you prefer it, modern Christianity and still be neither a pagan nor an infidel; while he may be inside it and not practice the things spoken of, by means of which he would be as much at variance with the requirements of our Father and Savior, perhaps, as the others named, and none of them be of necessity bad people, or among those wholly condemned."

"Then you believe in the actual practice of laying on of hands as well as of baptism by immersion?"

"Assuredly I do."

"And practice it, perhaps?"

"Whenever necessary, yes."

" Well, for fear you may not wish to try it here, and it is nearly bed time, I will relieve you of one of the 'devils,' and the power of 'casting out' can be held in reserve for some future occasion."

"My dear sir, you do us both injustice. No one would put you in such a category, and it is not a part of the work of a Christian to come into a circle as I have and engender harsh feelings, far from it."

"Oh, no matter. We might talk again at another time, when I may be pleased to continue our remarks, but not tonight as I only intended remaining a short time, having an important engagement which I was compelled to make since I saw you last evening ; so, if you will excuse me, I will wish you all good evening."

And so saying, the churchman, in not a very pleasant mood, withdrew.]

Said Brown : "Stranger, I am somewhat familiar with the doctrines of different Christian

societies, and from the way you expressed yourself regarding the personality of God, I would
like very much to hear your views regarding
other differences. If the rest of your views are
as reasonable as these you have given expression to, I should like very much to hear them,
and you can now proceed without interruption.
Do you differ from these ministers very much
in other principles?"

"I am afraid the difference on many very
important principles is just as great as the
difference concerning the personality of God.
But if you really desire to go with me in this
search after the kingdom of God, and the
others are willing, I assure you it will give me
great pleasure."

Unanimous approval was expressed at once,
and Mr. Brown continued, saying :

"I never before had as great a desire in this
direction, and must confess that my curiosity
has become quite aroused."

"Then," said Durant, "we will take King

James' translation of the Holy Scriptures as the law book, and 'Seek [ye first the kingdom of God' for our text; and if we should discover before we have finished that the teachings of men differ greatly from the teachings of Christ, I will be somewhat justified in saying that religionists have 'transgressed the laws, changed the ordinance, broken the everlasting covenant.'" (Isaiah xxiv: 5. Jeremiah ii: 13.)

"Very well," said Mr. Brown, "I will proceed," and obtaining the family Bible he continued: "And should your assertions prove correct, it might perhaps account for the increase of infidelity, and it might also cause others as well as myself to stop and consider. Now, then, to the 'law and the testimony.' Give me the chapter and verse, that I may know you make no mistake."

The doctor then for the first time took part, saying: "I am also becoming very much interested, and think I shall join you with my Bible. Let us all come into the circle."

"All right, we will examine the Gospel of
Jesus Christ from the Bible, principle by principle. In order to have a clear understanding
concerning this, it will be necessary for us to
go back to the days of our Father Adam.
Through the transgression of our first parents,
death came upon all the human family, and
mankind could not, of themselves, overcome
the same and obtain immortality. To substantiate this, see first, second and third chapters of
Genesis, Romans 5th chapter and 12th verse,
and I. Corinthians 15th chapter and 21st and
22nd verses. But in order that they should not
perish, God sent His Son Jesus Christ into the
world to satisfy this broken law and to deliver
mankind from the power of death. (John iii :
16 ; Romans v : 8 ; John iv: 9.) And as all
became subject to death by Adam, so will all
men be resurrected from death through the
atonement of Christ (I. Cor. xv : 20-23 ; Rom.
v : 12-19 ; Mark xvi: 15, 16), and will stand
before the judgment seat of God to answer for

their own sins and not for Adam's transgression. (Acts xvii : 31 ; Rev. xx : 12–15 ; Matt. xvi: 27.) Am I right as far as I have gone?"

"Yes," said the doctor, "I have been following you with your quotations, and find them correct. Proceed."

"Then I have proved one of the principles of some of the so-called Christians incorrect, for they do not believe that the wicked will have the same chance of resurrection as the righteous. Jesus Christ did not die for our individual sins, only on condition that we conform to the plan He has marked out, which will bring us a remission of our sins. The only way we can prove that we love Him is by keeping His commandments (John xiv : 15); therefore, if we say we love God and keep not His commandments, we are liars and the truth is not in us. (I. John ii : 4.) I think I have proved to your satisfaction that there is something defective with their understanding of the attributes of God, and I think I can prove also that they do not keep His commandments. Christ has given us to understand two things which you must remember while on this search after the 'kingdom of God.' First, that we must follow Him ; secondly, that when He left His disciples He was to send them the Comforter that would lead them into all truth ; therefore we must follow Christ and accept all the principles which were taught by His disciples while in possession of the Holy Spirit, though it should prove the world to be in error."

"Thus far your arguments are reasonable, also in accordance with Holy Writ; and as there is no other name given us except Jesus Christ whereby we can be saved (Acts iv : 12), you may now lay before us the conditions ; but give us chapter and verse, as I said before, that we may know you speak correctly."

"We will now examine into the conditions ; but first remember that God does not send men into the world for the purpose of preaching contrary doctrines, for this always creates confusion, and God is not the author of confusion, but of peace. (I. Cor. xiv: 33.) Paul has said, if any man teach another gospel let him be accursed. (Gal. i : 8, 9.) The first condition is this: To believe there is a God (not the kind mentioned in the English prayer book), but the God that created man in His own image, and to have faith in that God and in Jesus Christ whom He has sent.

"Go on," said the party in concert.

"Well," continued Durant, "the kind of faith required is that which will enable a man, under all circumstances, to say, 'I am not ashamed of the gospel of Christ ; for it is the power of God unto salvation.' (Rom. i: 16.) This is the kind of faith by which Noah prepared an ark ; by which the worlds were framed; by which the Red Sea was crossed as on dry land ; by which the walls of Jericho fell down ; it was by this faith that kingdoms were subdued ; righteousness was wrought; promises were obtained, and the mouths of lions were closed.

(Heb. xi: 32, 38.) This faith comes by hearing
the word of God (Rom. x: 14), and the lack of
this faith, and the absence of prayer and fast-
ing, caused even the apostles to be unsuccessful
on one occasion in casting out devils. (Matt.
xvii : 14, 20.) No wonder, then, that without
faith it is impossible to please God. (Heb. xi :
6.) Faith, then, is the first grand and glorious
stepping-stone to that celestial pathway leading
towards the eternal rest. The more we search
into eternal truth, the more we discover that
God works upon natural principles. All the
requirements which He makes of us are very
plain and simple. How natural that the principle of faith should be the primary one of our
salvation ! With what principle are we more
familiar? Faith is the first great principle
governing all things ; but great and grand as it
is, it is dead without works. (James ii: 14–
17.) We must not expect salvation by simply
having faith that Jesus is the Christ, for the
devils in purgatory are that far advanced (James

ii : 19.) In fact if you will read the entire second chapter of James you will see that faith without works is as dead and helpless as the body after the spirit has taken its departure. It is utter folly to think of gaining an exaltation in His presence unless we obey the principles He advocated (Matt. vii: 21), for no one speaks truthfully by saying he is a disciple of Christ while not observing His commandments. (John viii: 31.) In fact, the only way by which man can truthfully say he loves Jesus Christ is by keeping His commandments." (John xiv: · 12–21.)

"Is it not recorded in Holy Writ," said the doctor, "that if we believe in the Lord Jesus Christ we will be saved?"

"You have referred to the words used by Paul and Silas to the keeper of the prison. These disciples were asked by this keeper what he should do to be saved, and was assured, as you have quoted, 'Believe on the Lord Jesus Christ and thou shalt be saved, and thy house.'

Then the disciples immediately laid before them those principles which constituted true belief, and not until this man and his house had embraced the principles taught by these disciples were they filled with true belief and really rejoiced. (Acts xvi: 31–33.) You see by this example that we must not deceive ourselves by thinking that we can be hearers of the word only and not doers." (James i: 22, 23.)

"But, friend," said the lawyer, "here is a passage found in the tenth chapter of Romans, which, in my opinion, will be extremely hard for you to explain. The passage referred to reads as follows: 'If thou shalt confess with thy mouth the Lord Jesus, and shalt believe in thine heart that God hath raised Him from the dead, thou shalt be saved.' Now, then, it looks to me as if salvation is here promised through faith alone. How do you explain it?"

"Very easily. Let us thoroughly examine this passage in all its different phases. In the first place, this letter was written by Paul to individuals who were already members of the church. They had rendered obedience to the laws of salvation, and having complied with those requirements were entitled to salvation providing their testimony remained within them like a living spring ; and in order that they should not become lukewarm, Paul exhorted them to continue bearing testimony of the divinity of Christ, and not let their hearts lose sight of the fact that God had raised His Son from the dead, and inasmuch as they kept themselves in this condition, salvation would be theirs. This is the only sensible view one can take of this passage. Unquestionably, Paul was speaking to sincere members of the church, who had been correctly initiated into the folds of Christ, not aliens living 1800 years after."

" That appears to be correct, and is satisfactory ; but further on in the same chapter we find this expression: 'For whosoever shall call upon the name of the Lord shall be saved.' It appears to me here that reference is not made to those who had embraced the gospel and those who had the faith, but salvation is made general to whomsoever shall call upon the name of the Lord." (Rom. x: 13.)

"Exactly, but the next verse gives an explanation so simple that none can fail to understand it: 'How, then, shall they call on Him in whom they have not believed? and how shall they believe in him of whom they have not heard, and how shall they hear without a preacher? So, then, faith cometh by hearing, and hearing by the word of God.' In other words, if there is faith, there have been works, and having true faith, no person will remain in that condition without complying with further works of, salvation to which that faith urges him."

"I see, I see," said Brown, the others remaining silent, but interested; "you are right, but I never looked at the matter in that way before."

"Now, then, ladies and gentlemen," said Durant: "I maintain as before stated, that faith is the first principle of the gospel leading to salvation, but it will not bring us to the top of the glorious gospel ladder without the other principles."

"Well, suppose we accept this as the first round in the gospel ladder, where will we find the second?"

"To explain this question involves, perhaps, some little time, and as it must be near the 'witching hour' of midnight, I would not care to be responsible for extending the sitting beyond, or even up to, that time. To give this information is, in some measure, my errand among you, and if desired I shall be pleased to meet with you again. Before leaving I hope to be able to address the citizens publicly, and will do so if a suitable place can be obtained."

Both the doctor and the lawyer were disposed to remonstrate against adjournment, and there seemed to be none who were not willing to remain and hearken unto that which to them was

5

somewhat in the nature of an awakening, notwithstanding, as stated, it was growing late, and
the exercises had been purely colloquial. It
might be mentioned that only the more important
parts of the conversation have been produced
here—for the reproduction of everything in the
nature of mere colloquy, the auxilliary questions, answers and suggestions, would make
this a large book instead of a small one.
Besides, the full conversation would be no more
interesting for the particular object to which
this book is devoted than would the matter
reported.

The visitors took their departure with evident
regret, albeit their interest in the occasion was
more attributable to unsatisfied curiosity than
to concurrence in all that the stranger had said.

"He can talk Bible by the yard," said one.

"Yes, and show what it means better than a
regular minister," said another.

"He said he had a mission among us," chimed
in a third; "I wonder what it can be?"

The parting on the veranda was one in which friendly feelings prevailed all around, and the meeting on the morrow, when the second of the grand fundamental principles of the gospel was to be explained, seemed uppermost in every mind.

CHAPTER V.

FURTHER DISCUSSION OF THE FIRST PRINCIPLES.

THE audience had increased in numbers when the time for the continuance of the gospel exposition arrived.   Rev. Fitzallen was not present ; he had an engagement elsewhere, was the word he left ; but his absence was compensated for by the presence of two or three others.

But little time was spent in formality, and a beginning was effected by our legal friend saying :

"Mr. Durant, you closed last night with a definition of the first principle in the series of steps to be taken by the convert to Christianity, with a promise that tonight we should have the second explained.   Will you now proceed to fulfill the promise?"

"Most willingly, if it is desired."

Unanimous approval was at once manifested, and the western man proceeded.

"The second follows the first, just as naturally as the second step follows the first when a child learns to walk. When faith in God is once created, the knowledge that we have at some time, perhaps many times during our lives, done things displeasing to Him, naturally follows immediately, therefore repentance makes its appearance as the second principle of the gospel. When John came preaching in the wilderness, as the forerunner of Christ, his message to the people was, 'Repent ye : for the kingdom of heaven is at hand.' (Matt. iii : 2.) When Jesus came into Galilee preaching the gospel of the kingdom of God, it was with a message calling them to repentance. (Mark i : 15.) When He chose His disciples and began sending them forth, it was to call mankind to repentance. (Mark vi: 7-12.) When He upbraided the cities wherein the most of His mighty works were done, it was because they

repented not. (Matt. xi: 20.) True repentance is that which will cause him who
stole to steal no more ; that which will keep
corrupt communications from our mouths ; that
which will cause us to so conduct our walks
through life as not to grieve the Spirit of God ;
that which will cause all bitterness, wrath,
anger, and evil speaking to be put away from
us, and will make us kind one to another, ten-
der-hearted and forgiving even as God for
Christ's sake has forgiven us. (Ephesians iv :
28–32.) When he who has committed a sin
shall commit it no more, then he has repented
with that Godly sorrow which worketh repentance to salvation, and not with the sorrow of
the world, bringing with it death. (II. Cor.
vii : 10.) When a sinner repents with such
repentance more joy is found in heaven than
over ninety and nine just persons who need no
repentance. (Luke xv : 7.) This, then, ladies
and gentlemen, is the second round in the gospel ladder according to the plan given us by the

Master, and without it, faith is of no substantial consequence whatever."

"Your reasoning is both logical and just," said Brown, "and no one can find fault with those doctrines. This world of ours would certainly be more pleasant if these teachings were followed, and when a person is filled with that kind of faith, and has truly repented with such repentance, it must be manifest that he is entitled to salvation."

"But he must not stop at that," the speaker went on, "there are other principles just as important, just as necessary, for him to obey. If I am in possession of enough faith to convince me that I have sinned against you, and the knowledge of this causes me sincerely to repent, I must not and cannot rest until I am satisfied I have your forgiveness for the wrong. So it is with sinning against God and His laws; He has marked out the path of repentance and it is our duty to follow that divine way until we arrive at the sacred altar of forgiveness. Sin must be forgiven before it can be wiped out, and God in His wisdom selected and placed in His Church water baptism, as spoken of last night, for this purpose. It is a means whereby man can receive forgiveness of sin."

"And do you really believe that baptism brings forgiveness of sin?" queried the lawyer.

" Certainly, provided, however, honest faith and sincere repentance go before it, and the ordinance is administered in the proper way by one who is endowed with divine authority ; otherwise I believe it is of no avail whatever."

"It seems to me you surround the principle of baptism with more safeguards than anyone else of whom I have ever heard. Why so?"

"Perhaps I do, and yet it should not be the case. Every principle of the gospel should be well and carefully protected, and the failure on the part of man to do this is the main cause of so many different so-called plans of salvation existing among us today, when there should be only one true and perfect plan, as found in the days of Christ."

" You are certainly giving me ample information on religious conditions. It does seem strange that there should be so many different roads, leading, as is claimed, in one direction. I declare, I never thought of that before."

" Well, we will try to cover all .those points before we finish. Let us examine this principle. Let us see if the idea of water baptism appears reasonable. The Lord has wisely and kindly selected this form of ordinance for the remission of sins. It was with this object in view that John advocated the principle. (Mark i: 4.) Peter promised it on the day of Pentecost. (Acts ii: 38.) Saul also received aid to arise and have his sins washed away. (Acts xxii: 16.) And so it was taught by different disciples as a means whereby God would forgive sins."

"And as you have already stated, there are various modes of baptism among different sects. What is your method ?"

"The only correct form, as stated before, is that explained in the Bible. Baptism was performed anciently by immersion, in fact no other mode was thought of until centuries after the day of Christ. The word baptize is from the Greek *baptizo* or *bapto*, meaning to plunge or immerse, and such noted writers as Polybius, Strabo, Dion Cassius, Mosheim, Luther, Calvin, Bossuet, Schaaf, Baxter, Jeremy Taylor, Robinson, and others, all agree that with the ancients immersion, and no other form, was baptism. The holy record itself explains the mode so plainly that even a wayfaring man might understand. John selected a certain place on account of there being much water. (John iii: 23.) Christ Himself was baptized in a river, after which He came up out of the water. (Mark i: 5–10.) Both Philip and the eunuch went down into the water (Acts viii: 38, 39), and Paul likens baptism to the burial and resurrection of Christ, dying from sin, buried in water, and a resurrection to a new life. (Rom. vi: 3–5.)

Jesus declares that a man must be born of the water as well as of the spirit. (John iii: 5.) By being immersed we are born of the water, and we cannot liken baptism to a birth when performed in any other way. How mankind can accept any other form, in the face of all these facts, is more than I can account for. I think enough has been said to show that I am correct in my views regarding the object and mode of baptism, so now let us enquire who are proper subjects."

"Why, all who have souls to save, I suppose," said the doctor.

"Yes, providing they have obeyed the two principles, already mentioned; that is, faith and repentance ; for Christ commanded His apostles to teach before baptizing. (Matthew, xxviii: 19 and 20.) The candidate must believe before he can be baptized. (Mark xvi : 16.) Before Philip baptized the people of Samaria they believed the Gospel as he taught it. (Acts viii: 12.) When the eunuch asked for baptism at the hands

of this same disciple, Philip answered : ' If thou
believest with all thine heart, thou mayest.'
(Acts viii: 37.)   All persons, then, who are
capable of understanding, are fit subjects for
baptism as soon as they believe and have
repented.   None are exempt, not even was Cor-
nelius of old who was so generous that a report
of his good deeds reached the throne of God.
His prayers were so mingled with faith that
they brought down an angel from heaven ; yet
through baptism alone was it possible that he
could gain membership in the fold of Christ.
(Acts x.)   We see, then, that all, except little
children, are proper subjects for this ordinance,
providing, as stated, they have faith, and have
truly repented of their sins."

"And do you claim that little children are
exempt?" said the doctor.

"I do ; baptism is for the remission of sins,
and little children, being free from sin, are of
necessity exempt."

"I do not see how you make that doctrine

accord with the teachings of the Bible. Did not Jesus say, 'Suffer liltle children to come unto me?'"

"He did, but instead of administering the ordinance of baptism unto them, He took them in His arms and blessed them, declaring at the same time that they were pure and free from sin like unto those who were in the kingdom of heaven. A little child is free from sin, is pure in heart, humble and merciful, in fact is the great example of goodness which Christ points out for us to follow. (Mark x: 13-16.) This ordinance, then, is for people who are old enough to embrace it intelligently, not for children who cannot understand its significance, and who already belong to the kingdom of heaven.

"We have now examined three of the fundamental principles of the gospel of salvation. There is one more that I wish to touch upon, after which we will discuss a subject that is of more interest to you, perhaps, than any of these.

The principle which I wish to speak of now, is
the gift of the Holy Ghost, which in olden
times always followed the embracing of the
principles we have discussed, and when once received brought with it some of the gifts of the
gospel. When the first sermon was delivered
after the crucifixion of Christ, at the time when
the apostles were endowed with ·power from
on high, a multitude of people were pricked in
their hearts, and asked Peter and the rest of the
apostles what they should do. Peter undertook
to answer this all-important question, and so far
as authority to do so was concerned, we must
admit that he, of all men at that peculiar time,
was fully capable, for he was in possession of
the keys of the kingdom of God bestowed upon
him by Christ Himself. He was the chief
apostle and, with his brethren, had been endowed with power from above. Therefore, he,
more than any minister of our day, occupied a
place that enabled him to answer correctly, and
with authority."

"You are stating the case properly, but what did he tell them?" queried the interested man of law.

"His answer is found in the second chapter of Acts, beginning with the 38th verse. You will observe that as soon as he discovered that they had faith, he immediately taught them repentance, then baptism for the remission of sins, and followed these doctrines with a promise of the gift of the Holy Ghost.

"Yes, commencing at the verse mentioned it says: 'Then Peter said unto them, Repent and be baptized every one of you in the name of Jesus Christ for the remission of sins, and ye shall receive the gift of the Holy Ghost. For the promise is unto you, and to your children, and to all that are afar off, *even* as many as the Lord our God shall call.'"

"But how were they to receive the Holy Ghost?"

"By the laying on of hands. When Peter went down into Samaria for the purpose of bestowing this gift on those whom Philip had baptized, he did it by the laying on of hands. (Acts viii : 17.) Ananias conferred it upon Paul in the same manner (Acts ix : 17), and Paul did the same in the case of those who were baptized at Ephesus (Acts xix : 2-6) ; and when people received this birth of the Spirit (John iii : 5), they also received the promised blessings ; they were entitled to the signs which He promised would follow ; for said He, ' These signs shall follow them that believe ; in my name shall they cast out devils ; they shall speak with new tongues ; they shall take up serpents ; and if they drink any deadly thing it shall not hurt them ; they shall lay hands on the sick and they shall recover.' (Mark xvi : 17, 18.) We have now discovered the conditions : faith, repentance, baptism for the remission of sins, and the laying on of hands for the reception of the Holy Ghost, with the promise of Christ that the signs will follow. Can you tell me now, which of all these different denomi-

nations has the gospel 'of Jesus Christ ?   Or as
Wesley has questioned in one of his hymns
which we may with profit quote in full : 'Show
me where true Christians live.'"

"Happy the souls that first believ'd,
To Jesus and each other cleav'd,
Joined by the unction from above,
In mystic fellowship of love.

"Meek, simple foll'wers of the Lamb,
They liv'd, and spake, and thought the same;
They joyfully conspir'd to raise
Their ceaseless sacrifice of praise.

"With grace abundantly endued,
A pure believing multitude;
They all were of one heart and soul,
And only love inspir'd the whole.

"Oh, what an age of golden days!
Oh, what a choice, peculiar race!
Wash'd in the Lamb's all-cleansing blood,
Anointed kings and priests to God.

"Where shall I wander now to find
Successors they have left behind?
The faithful, whom I seek in vain,
Are 'minish'd from the sons of men.
6

"Ye diff'rent sects, who all declare,
'Lo, here is Christ,' or 'Christ is there!'
Your stronger proofs divinely give,
And show me where the Christians live."

"You must remember, my friend, that the signs were only given in order to establish the church in the day of the apostles, but now they are abrogated and are no longer needed."

"'To the law and to the testimony,'" replied Durant "and give me chapter and verse to substantiate the assertion you have just made."

"If you will read the 13th chapter of the 1st Corinthians, you will learn that 'whether there be prophecies they shall fail, and whether there be tongues they shall cease.'"

"If you will take pains to read the two verses following, you will see that 'we know in part, and we prophesy in part. But when that which is perfect is come, then that which is in part shall be done away.' My friend, instead of this quotation proving that these things are done away, it establishes the assertion that they shall remain until perfection shall come. Surely no sane man will say that we have come to perfection."

"I have understood that these gifts were no longer needed. This certainly is the conclusion the ministers of the day have come to."

"But this is not surprising to me, for this good old Bible declares that the time will come when the people will turn from sound doctrine to fables." (II. Tim. iv : 4.)

"I must admit that you have convinced me that baptism is a necessity, and when I am baptized, the ordinance will be performed in the proper manner," said the doctor.

"I am pleased to learn that, but I may have another surprise for you yet. May I ask, who do you intend shall baptize you ?"

"My minister, I suppose ; why ?"

"If the words of the Bible be true, there may be a doubt as to whether your minister is authorized to baptize you."

"Do you mean to prove that these men, min-

isters of the gospel, have no authority to offici-
ate in that ordinance ?   I wonder what you will
undertake next, but proceed, for I am now prepared for surprises."

"I assure you, my dear sir, I only wish to
refer to a few doctrines from the Bible which
are necessary to be understood by you in order
that you may obtain eternal life.   Thus far we
have only examined the first principles of the
gospel, but now we will speak of the officers
whom Christ placed in His Church, and learn
by what means men receive authority to act in the
name of God.   Paul tells us that God has placed
'first apostles, secondarily prophets, thirdly
teachers, after which gifts of healing,' etc. (I.
Cor. xii : 28), and says the work is built upon
the foundation of apostles.   (Eph. ii : 20.) He
furthermore declares that these officers have
been placed in the Church for the work of the
ministry, and to remain until we all come to a
knowledge of the truth. (Eph. iv : 11-13). Have
all mankind come to a knowledge of the truth ?

If not, why has the church dispensed with the
officers that God placed in it for the purpose of
bringing all to a unity of the faith ? Paul tells
us that these officers were placed in the Church
to keep us from being tossed to and fro and
carried about by every wind of doctrine which
is taught by man. (Eph. iv : 12-14.) At the
present time, when men declare that they have
no need of apostles or prophets, they are divided, and subdivided, and in fact carried about
by every doctrine that is promulgated—as Paul
saw that they would be, if inspired apostles and
prophets were not found to lead them. In losing these officers, the Church lost her authority,
together with all her gifts and graces, and the
so-called Christian churches today are disrobed
of all her beautiful garments ; and even those
who pretend to defend her are crying out that
her gifts, graces and ordinances are useless in
this age of the world. Did Christ establish the
true order or did He not ? We say He did, and
would ask, has any man a right to change it ?

And if any man or even an angel from heaven should alter it in the least, will he not come under the condemnation that Paul uttered when he said : 'Though we or an angel from heaven preach any other gospel unto you than that which we have preached unto you, let him be accursed?' (Gal. i : 8.) Christ placed these officers and the ordinances in the Church for the perfection of the Saints ; and any one teaching contrary to this is a perverter of the gospel, and an anti-Christ in the full meaning of the word. The difference between the true Church of Christ on the one hand, and the Catholic Church, with all her posterity composing the whole protestant world on the other hand, amounts to this : one had apostles, prophets, etc., who led the Church by inspiration or by divine revelation ; while the others have learned men to preach learned men's opinions ; have colleges to teach divinity instead of the Holy Ghost ; instead of preaching the gospel without hire, their ministers must have large salaries each year, and they are not certain of the doctrines which they teach, when they should be in possession of the gifts of knowledge, prophecy and revelation. Now then in what church do we find apostles and prophets ?"

The doctor replied, "There are none ; but you must remember there must be a preacher, for 'how shall they hear without a preacher ?'" (Rom. x : 14.)

" And in the next verse he asks, ' How shall they preach except they be sent?' This same apostle says that no man is to take the honor unto himself, but he that is called of God as was Aaron. (Heb. v : 4.) Aaron was called by revelation (Ex. iv: 14-17) ; hence we see that no man is to preach the gospel except he be called by revelation from God. As I said, instead of men being called by revelation—as the Bible declares they should be—in our day they argue that God has not revealed Himself for almost eighteen hundred years. Go and ask your minister if he has been called by revela-

tion, and he will tell you that such manifestations are not needed now, which assertion I
think will prove to you that he has no authority
to baptize for the remission of sins."

"But did not Jesus say, 'Go ye into all the
world and preach the gospel?'"

"He did; but was He talking to modern
ministers then? When He gave His apostles
authority to preach, did that give all men who
feel disposed to take the honor unto themselves,
the same authority? He gave His apostles to
understand that they had not chosen Him, but
He had chosen them (John xv : 16); but in this
day men reverse the condition. Then again,
He sent His servants into the world to preach
His gospel without purse or scrip. (Luke x : 4.)
Paul says his reward is this, 'That when I
preach the gospel I may make the gospel of
Christ without charge, that I abuse not my
power in the gospel.' (I. Cor. ix : 18.) Now, go
and ask your minister if he does the same, and
I think you will find that he must have a salary."

"Then what has become of the gospel?" said the lawyer.

"Paul says that the coming of Jesus Christ will not be, save there be 'a falling away' (II. Thess. ii : 3), and that 'in the last days perilous times shall come.' (II. Tim. iii : 1.) People 'will not endure sound doctrine,' but will 'heap to themselves teachers having itching ears, and shall turn from the truth to fables (II. Tim. iv : 3, 4), and will have a form of godliness but will deny the power thereof. (II. Tim. iii : 5.) Peter also says these false teachers will make merchandise of the souls of men. (II. Peter ii : 1-3.) They are doing so by demanding a salary for preparing sermons to tickle the people's itching ears. Micah (iii : 11) says, their heads judge for reward, their priests teach for hire, and their prophets divine for money, yet they lean upon the Lord and say, is not the Lord among us ? Now, my friends, do not the different sects of the day present us with a literal fulfillment of all these sayings ? Have they not transgressed

the laws, changed the ordinance and broken the
everlasting covenant? (Isaiah xxiv : 5.) John
Wesley in his 94th sermon, referring to the
condition of the church after it had departed
from the right way and lost the gifts, says :
' The real cause why the extraordinary gifts
of the Holy Ghost were no longer to be
found in the Christian Church was because the
Christians were turned heathens again and had
only a dead form left."

"It would appear, then, that God has forsaken
mankind and left us without any hope," said Mr.
Marshall.

"No, he has not ; but this falling away, is
the result of mankind forsaking God, by
changing His gospel and departing from its
teachings, as I have already shown. But He
has promised, through his servants, that there
would be a dispensation when He would gather
together all things in Christ (Eph. i: 10), and
would restore all things which He has spoken
by the mouth of all His holy Prophets since the

world began. (Acts iii : 20, 21.) This dispensation was called the dispensation of the fullness of times. (Eph. i : 10.) Daniel, who
received, by revelation, the interpretation of
Nebuchadnezzar's dream, saw what would take
place in the latter times, when the God of
heaven would set up a kingdom. (Dan. ii : 44.)
John, the revelator, while on that desolate island
Patmos (some ninety years after Christ), saw
how this gospel would be restored: namely,
that an angel would bring it from heaven (Rev.
xiv : 6), and Christ says it 'shall be preached
in all the world as a witness unto all nations;
and then shall the end come.' (Matt. xxiv: 14.)
As God is always the same, and has but one
plan for the redemption of the human family,
we may expect to see the same gospel with like
promises preached in a similar way. Where do
we find it as it existed anciently? But as it was
in the days of Noah, so shall it be also in the
days of the coming of the Son of Man. (Matt.
xxiv: 37; Luke xvii: 26, 27.) Noah was sent

by the Lord to foretell the coming of the flood,
but the people rejected his testimony, in fact,
whenever God has revealed His mind and will
to man in days gone by, the world, instead of
receiving the same, have rejected the message
and said all manner of evil concerning the
prophets, and in many instances have killed
them, as was the case with Christ Himself.
Now then, my friends, we are living in the dispensation of the fullness of times, when God
is gathering together all things in Christ. An
angel has come from the heavens and brought
the everlasting gospel, and on the 6th day of
April, 1830, God—through revelation to man—
organized the kingdom spoken of by Daniel, in
the exact pattern of the kingdom as it existed
in the days of Christ, with apostles and prophets,
and since that day the servants of God have
been traveling through the world preaching the
same, as a witness that the end will soon come.
They call upon mankind to exercise faith in God
our eternal Father, and in His Son Jesus Christ,

also to repent of, and turn from their sins, and be baptized by one who has been called of God by revelation, and receive the laying on of hands for the bestowal of the Holy Ghost. As servants of God they then promise that the convert shall know of the doctrine, whether it be of God or man (John vii: 17); and, furthermore, that the signs which followed the believers in the days of the ancient apostles will follow the believer at the present time, for the same cause will always produce the same effect. My friends, as a servant of God, I call upon you to obey these principles and you shall have the promised blessings."

The doctor said: "Much that you say is convincing, some of it excites curiosity, and all is entertaining. I will now announce that the Town Hall has been obtained for Saturday night and as that involves a little longer stay than you intended, I suggest that a collection be taken and turned over to you."

"I beg you, do nothing of that kind," said

the missionary. "If the hall is free, the lecture
shall be also; and I can doubtless spend the
time pleasantly enough till then."

"Very well, if that is your pleasure. There
will be such an attendance as this town has
rarely seen, I promise you."

And then after a few pleasantries in the
usual vein, and a general "good night," the
party separated just as the clock struck twelve,
each in the best humor.

In view of the coming lecture it was mutually
agreed that the veranda gatherings should be
discontinued for the present at least.

CHAPTER VI.

TRUTH AGAIN DEFEATS FALSEHOOD.

THE meeting was to be held in the Town
Hall on Saturday, and in the meantime our
missionary busied himself variously, but devoted
part of the time in getting his lecture arranged
and in refreshing his memory on the topics upon
which he wished to speak. When not thus
employed he took strolls about the country, or
engaged in pleasant bits of conversation with
his acquaintances, and with others whom he
happened to meet on the way. He was such a
favorite at the Marshall mansion that the people
there were always pleased to have him express
a wish for anything, in order that it might at
once be gratified; but such expressions were
very rare and confined to the scope of his actual
requiremeuts.

On Friday afternoon he engaged in a pleasant

discussion with Mrs. Marshall on some scriptural topic.   Missionaries all understand the
power of song, Mr. Durant was no exception,
so at one point he sang one of his hymns:

> " How the light from Zion's mountain
>   Clears the mists of error's age:
> Clarified in ray and fountain,
>   How its truths our fears assuage!

> " Tempest-tossed, we still are certain
>   Life is but a pleasant span.
> Hope has painted every curtain
>   Pictured in the gospel plan.

> " Once again to every nation,
>   Jesus opens wide the door;
> Here are truths that bring salvation,
>   Preached and practiced as of yore.

> " Joyful tidings to the people
>   From the perfect courts on high;
> Sweetest chimes from tower and steeple
>   Ring: Redemption's drawing nigh.

> " Shine, thou light, with doubled splendor,
>   Spread thy soothing, restful rings,
> Till the sun of Zion, tender
>   Rise, with healing in his wings!"

The daughter was an interested listener, and at the close broke in with—"It seems to me that there is no such thing as perfect happiness after all. We are always being disappointed in relation to some hope or desire, and when we engage in that which affords pastime or amusement, there is invariably a penalty following. Is not this true, Mr. Durant?"

"I could scarcely dispute with a lady, even if there were grounds for it," said he, gallantly.

"But I prefer you would," she said, "because you appear to know all about these things and I desire to learn. Why is it, for instance, that after enjoying myself greatly at a dance or other late entertainment, injured nature afterward cries out for revenge, and takes it? So with all things it seems to me. The pleasure experienced in meeting a dear friend is beclouded by the knowledge that there must be a parting soon; and death is ever near as if to remind us of the fact that life, happiness, honor,

7

wealth, youth, are all fleeting and unsubstantial."

" Very true."

" Why Claire," said her mother, " you are becoming a regular pessimist. Surely at your age there is no need to borrow trouble about death or anything else."

"I do not borrow it, mamma, it comes. Pain follows pleasure, sorrow treads upon the heals of happiness, and misfortune is the constant attendant of fortune. There is, as I said, no perfect happiness, so it seems to me."

" Pardon me," said the missionary, " but you did not finish your sentence. Shall I do so for you ?"

" O, by all means," replied the girl with eager delight.

" Well, then," he continued, " doubtless what you meant to say was that there is no such thing as perfect happiness in either the contemplation or realization of things which in themselves are fleeting and unsubstantial—that is, the things of the world. Every movement of the machinery of a steamer, for instance, creates friction, which in turn indicates an eventual breaking down, and so it is with all temporal things ; thus we cannot rely upon them for permanent good, and in addition they are constantly subjecting us to peril.

" It is impossible to create perfect results out of imperfect conditions ; therefore, there can be no complete or unbroken happiness come out of earthly surroundings, for the reason that all such things are changeable and fleeting. And yet there is such a state as perfect joy unclouded and endless."

" But not in this life, as you yourself have shown."

" Yes, in this life."

" I thought you referred to this life as uncertain and ephemeral and as such curtailed or extinguished its own joys."

" That is true, also. But yet endless and supreme delight is to be found in it."

"Where and how, pray?"

"In observing principles and practicing truths which lead to immortality, and which confer upon us the title-deeds to homes where pains and penalties are unknown, where all is peace, contentment and love."

"Oh, yes, I did not think of that."

"In such enjoyment there is no alloy. More than that; the more it is engaged in, the more enjoyable it becomes; it does not cloy, we cannot become surfeited; the more we devote our attention and effort to it the greater the desire we have to continue and to increase our experience. This is that perfect happiness with which nothing else can compare."

"But would you have us dispense with all pleasures—with the refined indulgences, the innocent pastimes and the intellectual recreations which lighten our burdens at least for the time being, and have us participate in sacred things only? Should there be no buoyancy of spirit, no diversion, no relaxation, in order that there might be no penalty as the result of indulgence?"

"Why, what an—pardon me—absurd idea! Of course you do not advance it seriously and should therefore be free from criticism. Rather than that such a rule of conduct as you have suggested is the proper one, it is almost as bad as that in which amusement alone prevails. The medium course, which enables us to enjoy all that is properly enjoyable in its appropriate season, and still does not cause us to loose sight of the great aim and end of existence, is the right one. We should let our pastimes be the incidents in our career, not the objects of it; thus they lighten our burdens, and, for the time being, dispel some of the shadows that cross our pathway, whereas, if made the purpose of living—the only things to be considered—they become burdensome and even sinful."

"Then the devout Christian may be happy and jovial without being less a Christian, on account of that?"

"Yes, indeed. More—it is pleasing to our Father for His children to be light-hearted, so long as their pleasures are proper and are enjoyed in moderation. The people from among whom I come enjoy themselves as much as other people do, but do not overlook their devotions, and above all they remember the Sabbath day, to keep it holy."

"That seems to me," said Mrs. Marshall, "to be a sensible form of Christianity. Why, a person, according to your faith, can be profoundly religious and yet deny himself no proper amusement."

"Most decidedly ; that is our belief and practice."

"It seems to me I would like to be a member of your Church," said the girl, artlessly, at which interesting stage of the conversation, Rev. Fitzallan entered, who greeted the party stiffly, his brow having a distinct frown as he looked at the westerner.

"Pardon me," said the Clergyman, after a

few commonplaces had passed, "but we 'gather wisdom by the wayside,' and I have just acquired some information from that source concerning our friend here from the wilds, and as it surprised me, I thought it might equally surprise the rest of you, himself included, perhaps."

Evidently the churchman had been engaged in the questionable calling of picking up stray scraps of gossip here and there, containing as usual some truth mixed with much error. There was obviously trouble ahead.

"Anything concerning me is not apt to be of sufficient consequence to be very interesting," said Mr. Durant, "and having already stated all I thought worth saying about myself and my errand, there can be little or nothing that is surprising, I am sure."

"Is it not a fact that you are from Salt Lake City?"

"It is."

"It is! Why you never informed us of this

and yet you have been associated with us several days."

"Indeed! May I ask you, Mrs. Marshall, and you, Miss Marshall, what part of the country our friend here comes from ?"

The ladies did not know.

"Indeed! Why sir, you have been associated with this family several weeks, and yet they do not know what particular point you came from. Perhaps like myself, you were never asked."

"This is evasion," said the now thoroughly excited churchman. "There is no place in my district possessed of such peculiar conditions as would place one of its inhabitants under suspicion because of them."

"Nor in mine either, that I know of," calmly rejoined Durant.

"Is not Salt Lake City the headquarters and residence of a class of people known as Mormons who hold exclusive sway there ?" ·

"No, sir."

"That is what I have heard."

"Surely, I am not accountable for what you have heard. There are a great many Mormons in Salt Lake, and just as many that are not Mormons ; it is the headquarters of the Church as you suggest, but its members are not in exclusive sway there."

"How can that be ?"

"No matter about the means ; the fact itself is what concerns us."

The churchman was discomfited and measurably confused ; he was compelled to change his course.

"You told us," said he, that you were an advocate of the Church of Jesus Christ ; should there not be a suffix in these words—Latter-day Saints?"

"That is correct."

"And is not 'Mormonism' its other name ?"

"No, it has no other name. It is called 'Mormonism' by nearly every one not connected with it, and yet that is not a proper designation."

"Then to yourself you are a 'Latter-day Saint,' and to the world you are a 'Mormon?'"

"That is it exactly."

"Strange that we should be kept in ignorance of it so long."

"I have answered every question fairly and in addition have stated everything necessary to a full explanation of my cause and myself. If the doctrine I teach be true—and it has stood all tests so far—can you find nothing more than a name to oppose it?"

"I hope sir, you do not accuse me of innuendo?"

"I accuse you of nothing."

"Come now," said Mrs. Marshall, "do not be too earnest."

"Well, madam," said Rev. Fitzallan, "I thought my services in this connection would be received graciously and thankfully. As they are not I occupy the position of an intruder and will take my leave."

"Not on my account, I hope," said Mr. Durant. "If there is an intruder here it is I, and it would be my duty to depart."

"You must not go under such circumstances," said Mrs. Marshall.

The girl's looks seconded her mother's words, and the irate churchman permitted his passion to overcome his judgment.

"Excuse me," he said, "but I will take my leave. Under the circumstances my presence must be altogether unwelcome. I have heard of the fascinating character of some of the features of Mormonism, and the persuasiveness of those who advocate it. Violation of the laws of God and man by practicing polygamy is one of the seductive usages of that creed, I believe."

"Your belief is erroneous, then," said Durant. "Whatever my people may have believed in the past as to the correctness of doctrines taught by the Bible and the prophets of old, they now obey the laws of the land in which they live."

"Marvelous! I have heard otherwise. I

have even taken the pains to bring with me a
newspaper which I received from a traveler,
and in which information of a different character is obtained. It is published in Salt Lake
City and should be correct. Here is part of a
sermon delivered by a Mormon Bishop ; and
here an account of several arrests for violating
the law against polygamy and kindred offenses,
while an editorial in the same paper comments
strongly on the deception and falsity pervading
the Mormon people. There must be a mistake
somewhere."

" No, there is no mistake at all, but much
falsehood and misrepresentation. It is true
that since the law against polygamy was enacted
there have been many prosecutions of members
of our Church chiefly because of their inability
instantly to sever the happy associations of a
lifetime which had been formed before the law
went into effect, or their lack of exact knowledge as to what the law required of them. It
was a difficult, I may say an impossible matter,

for them to break away entirely from a part of
their families and never go near them, to give
a word of counsel, or it may be hurriedly to
embrace the little ones from whom the law had
separated them. When thus found they have
been apprehended, tried, convicted and punished,
often without an effort to defend themselves.
The Bishop named by the paper, does not, and
never did exist, and the sermon referred to
was never delivered, as the same paper has been
compelled to admit on several occasions; and
the editor's views, or rather sayings, are the
words of a man whose chief interest in the
community is to fan the flames of discord so
that his nefarious business may prosper. His
statements are utterly and entirely false."

After these remarks the reverend went to his
room, and shortly afterward took his departure.

" I don't like the Mormons at all, and I'm just
sorry you're one," said the girl.

" I too, am somewhat opposed to that peculiar
religion, but it does seem to me, after hearing

you, that my dislike arises more from prejudice than from anything else," said the mother.

"I have here a card containing the articles of our faith from which you may learn that we are not so evil as we are represented to be."

We believe in God, the Eternal Father, and in His Son, Jesus Christ, and in the Holy Ghost.

We believe that men will be punished for their own sins, and not for Adam's transgression.

We believe that, through the atonement of Christ, all mankind may be saved, by obedience to the laws and ordinances of the Gospel.

We believe that these ordinances are: First, Faith in the Lord Jesus Christ; second, Repentance; third, Baptism by immersion for the remission of sins; fourth, Laying on of Hands for the Gift of the Holy Ghost.

We believe that a man must be called of God, by "prophecy, and by the laying on of hands," by those who are in authority, to preach the gospel and administer in the ordinances thereof.

We believe in the same organization that existed in the primitive church, namely: apostles, prophets, pastors, teachers, evangelists, etc.

We believe in the gift of tongues, prophecy, revelation, visions, healing, interpretation of tongues, etc.

We believe the Bible to be the word of God, as far as it is translated correctly; we also believe the Book of Mormon to be the word of God.

We believe all that God has revealed, all that He does now reveal, and we believe that He will yet reveal many great and important things pertaining to the Kingdom of God.

We believe in the literal gathering of Israel and in the restoration of the Ten Tribes. That Zion will be built upon this continent. That Christ will reign personally upon the earth, and that the earth will be renewed and receive its paradisiacal glory.

We claim the privilege of worshiping Almighty God according to the dictates of our conscience, and allow all men the same privilege, let them worship how, where, or what they may.

We believe in being subject to kings, presidents, rulers and magistrates, in obeying, honoring and sustaining the law.

We believe in being honest, true, chaste, benevolent, virtuous, and in doing good to all men; indeed we may say that we follow the admonition of Paul, "We believe all things, we hope all things," we have endured many things, and hope to be a le to endure all things. If there is anything virtuous, lovely, or of good report, or praiseworthy, we seek after these, things.—*Joseph Smith.*

With this Durant took from his pocket the card, and handing it to Mrs. Marshall, said:

"Examine it at your leisure." And without more adieu he was gone, leaving the ladies in reflective mood.

Mr. Marshall received the news regarding Durant, in silence; perhaps he had suspected, or even knew already, that the stranger was a " Mormon."

CHAPTER VII.   ·

A TRIUMPH AND AN ESCAPE.

THE afternoon preceding the night on which Charles Durant was to appear before the public in the Town Hall of Westminster to place the plan of salvation before the people, and bear his testimony to the eternal truth, was wearing slowly away. By this time his name was on everybody's lips, and nearly all knew him. As he walked abroad some would pass him with a frown, some with a gaze of curiosity, rarely one would smile, and less frequently still would he receive a pleasant "good-day." If he had delighted in notoriety, here was certainly a field in which he might enjoy that to the full limit of his desire; but he wanted nothing of the kind. He was filled with the spirit of his calling which was to spread the truth and labor unto the salvation of men; and neither the insults of

the insolent nor the frowns of opponents could
turn him aside from that purpose. He bore
within his breast the realization of an upright
purpose, together with the certainty of a reward to come. What were threats and annoy-
ances to him? And yet he sought not persecution that a cheap martyrdom might be gained;
perhaps if warned of a personal danger, in obedience to a natural impulse, he would have
shunned or gone around it, but never to the
sacrifice of one jot or tittle of principle.

His experience of less than a week in Westminster had been sufficient for a volume of
much greater proportions than this little publi-
cation, and yet enough of it is noted here to
give a fair idea of what transpired. In that
time our hero, a comparative stranger, had become well-settled and was welcome in an honorable household, and this without deception or
any special effort to please; he had dethroned
the demon of infidelity in one good man's heart
when a skilled churchman's efforts in that di-

8

rection only threatened to perpetuate the evil; had caused another good man, indifferent to gospel measures, to become actively interested; had defeated the churchman spoken of, on his own ground, and had shown in an unmistakeable manner the fallacy of his doctrine, and finally, had brought this showy patron of religion to utter discomfiture without desiring, intending, or trying to annoy him in any way; had set the family named and several of their neighbors to thinking as they had never thought before; and now, as a special favor was to address the town people in their chief public building. The Town Hall was filled to overflowing, and when Durant entered and walked slowly up to the platform, it is perhaps needless to say he was the observed of all observers. There were some feelings of surprise when Mr. Brown, the (late) infidel, arose to introduce the speaker of the evening; he announced before doing so that the lecture would consist of an exposition of the groundwork, and some advanced .principles of

the gospel as laid down in the Bible. "Nothing will be left to be conjectured or surmised,"
he said; "the speaker is familiar with the subject and is capable of doing it justice. I speak
advisedly, having heard him before. I ask
your earnest and respectful attention, and now
present to you Mr. Charles Durant, of Salt
Lake City."

Notwithstanding the sacredness of the occasion, there was a burst of applause when
the speaker arose. Before him, on a table, were
the Bible and two or three other books. He
entered upon his subject at once, first explaining the principles of faith, repentance and
baptism, citing the Holy Book in support of
his arguments, and making every principle
plain and lucid as he proceeded. In as extended
a manner as he could, within the time at his
disposal, he developed the philosophy and
practice of true Christianity from the beginning to the present time, leaving no salient
point unmentioned, and no stone marking the

way, unturned. He occupied two hours, and there was not a listener but gladly would have remained that much longer. The impression made was deep; as to whether or not it was lasting, that depended largely upon the individuals themselves.

The lawyer and the doctor and the Marshalls came forward and grasped the speaker's hand extending sincere congratulations. The preacher was absent. As they left the room, people could be heard making such remarks as— "Well, that is mighty sound reasoning no matter where it comes from;" a few asked to be introduced and one of these, an old lady, said in a low voice, "You spoke the truth, I know it; God bless you!"

As soon as he could make his way to Durant's side, the negro, Cæsar, said hurriedly—"You want to look a little out as you go home; I heard a lot of fellers down the lane talking, and they said they would fix that Mormon." •

A spontaneous exclamation of surprise and

disgust came from the little party of which Durant was the center. However, it was left to the lawyer to engage in explosiveness, and he did it in a manner which left no doubt of what he would do in an emergency. It was finally decided that he and the doctor should lead the way homeward, with the Marshall family, our guest, a neighbor and the negro, following leisurely after. The improvised mob was soon encountered and the interview was stormy for awhile, but before the party in the rear reached the spot, the tumult was quieted down considerably. The lawyer knew every one in the party and if any violence was offered to the stranger, he would make it his personal business to see that every one of them answered to the law. This, coupled with milder and more persuasive methods, had its effect, and one by one the rioters dispersed, at least for the present. Mr. Durant and his friends walked home without being assaulted by so much as an unpleasant exclamation though he fully expected trouble from the first ; but he determined to continue his labor as he had begun, leaving the result to Providence.

CHAPTER VIII.

THE PROPHET JOSEPH'S STATEMENT.

PERHAPS it was the force of habit as well as the impelling power of desire that caused the group, with whom we are now so familiar, again to assemble at the place made somewhat memorable by recent events—the verandah fronting the Marshall mansion. All the persons hitherto named, excepting, of course, the minister, were present; that gentleman had not only taken his departure from the house, but doubtless from the town also.

It was Sunday evening, the weather was perfect, all things seemed conducive to harmony, and a most pleasurable occasion, it being perhaps the last they would enjoy together. The doctor and lawyer were so anxious to begin the conversation that they could scarcely wait for all to be seated ; they desired to improve the opportunity, and learn what they could of other principles of the missionary's faith.

"Mr. Durant," finally said the doctor, "we have listened with much pleasure to different conversations with you since your arrival and these have awakened a lively interest within us, and as there is nothing to prevent this evening, we thought it would not be at all unpleasant to you to spend an hour or so in answering what to us appears to be some very important questions concerning the faith of the so-called Mormons."

"I assure you it will be pleasant to me, indeed. I am here for that purpose, and the more questions I have an opportunity to answer, the better and more successfully will I perform my duty. Could I read your thoughts and know what you desire explained, I assure you nothing would be left untold ; but this not being the case, I rely upon you to make enquiries and will request that you keep nothing back, and I will be honest in giving any information that I am capable of imparting."

"I am now inclined to believe," said the doctor, "after our experience with you, that, like most of the good people of this nation we have been in possession of only one side of the question regarding your people. Never having heard, from your standpoint, the claims of Mr. Joseph Smith, the founder of your Church, in regard to his being a prophet, we would be pleased to learn what he said on this question."

"This is a frankness which I appreciate very much. As a general thing, the majority of the people, when desirous of knowing anything concerning us, are prone to ask any other person on earth than a Mormon. They do not seem to think for a moment that we ourselves might be able to place them in possession of the most reliable information on the subject. Joseph Smith's claim to being divinely inspired to open up a new dispensation of the gospel, is here given in his own statement so that you will be getting it direct from the fountain head."

"By all means, read it," said two or three in concert; "there will then be no room for mis-representation."

"Joseph Smith has made the following state-ment regarding the subject," continued Durant:

"Owing to the many reports which have been put in circu-lation by evil designing persons in relation to the rise and pro-gress of the Church of Jesus Christ of Latter-day Saints, all of which have been designed by the authors thereof to mili-tate against its character as a Church, and its progress in the world, I have been induced to write this history, so as to dis-abuse the public mind, and put all inquirers a'ter truth in possession of the facts as they have transpired in relation both to myself and the Church so far as I have such facts in pos-session.

"In this history I will present the various events in relation to this Church, in truth and righteousness, as they have transpired, or as they at present exist, being now the eighth year since the organization of the said Church.

"I was born in the year of our Lord one thousand eight hundred and five, on the twenty-third day of December, in the town of Sharon, Windsor County, State of Vermont. My father, Joseph Smith, senior, left the State of Vermont, and moved to Palmyra, Ontario (now Wayne) County, in the State of New York, when I was in my tenth year. In about four years after my father's arrival at Palmyra, he moved with his family into Manchester, in the same County of

Ontario. His family consisted of eleven souls, namely: my father, Joseph Smith, my mother, Lucy Smith (whose name previous to her marriage was Mack, daughter of Solomon Mack), my brothers Alvin (who is now dead), Hyrum, myself, Samuel Harrison, William, Don Carlos, and my sisters Sophronia, Catherine, and Lucy.

"Some time in the second year after our removal to Manchester, there was in the place where we lived an unusual excitement on the subject of religion. It commenced with the Methodists, but soon became general among all the sects in that region of country; indeed the whole district of country seemed affected by it, and great multitude united themselves to the different religious parties, which created no small stir and division amongst the people, some crying, Lo, here, and some, Lo there; some were contending for the Methodist faith, some for the Presbyterian, and some for the Baptists'. For notwithstanding the great love which the converts for these different faiths expressed at the time of their conversion, and the great zeal manifested by their respected clergy, who were active in getting up and promoting this extraordinary scene of religious feeling, in order to have everybody converted, as they were pleased to call it, let them join what sect they pleased: yet when the converts began to file off, some to one party, and some to another, it was seen that the seemingly good feelings of both the priests and the converts were more pretended than real, for a scene of great confusion and bad feeling ensued—priest contending against priest, and convert against convert, so that all the good feelings one for another, if they ever had any, were entirely lost in a strife of words, and a contest about opinions.

"I was at this time in my fifteenth year. My father's family was proselyted to the Presbyterian faith, and four of them joined that church, namely, my mother, Lucy, my brothers Hyrum, Samuel Harrison, and my sister Sophronia.

"During this time of great excitement, my mind was called up to serious reflection and great uneasiness; but though my feelings were deep and often pungent, still I kept myself aloof from all those parties, though I attended their several meetings as often as occasion would permit; but in process of time my mind became somewhat partial to the Methodist sect, and I felt some desire to be united with them, but so great was the confusion and strife among the different denominations, that it was impossible for a person, young as I was, and so unacquainted with men and things, to come to any certain conclusion who was right, and who was wrong. My mind at different times was greatly excited, the cry and tumult was so great and incessant. The Presbyterians were most decided against the Baptists and Methodists, and used all their powers of either reason or sophistry to prove their errors, or, at least, to make the people think they were in error. On the other hand the Baptists and Methodists, in their turn, were equally zealous to establish their own tenets and disprove all others.

"In the midst of this war of words and tumult of opinions, I often said to myself, What is to be done? Who of all these parties are right? Or, are they all wrong together? If any one of them be right, which is it, and how shall I know it?

"While I was laboring under the extreme difficulties, caused by the contests of these parties of religionists, I was one day reading the Epistle of James, first chapter, and fifth verse, which reads, If any of you lack wisdom, let him ask of God, that giveth unto all men liberally and upbraideth not, and it shall be given him. Never did any passage of scripture come with more power to the heart of man than this did at this time to mine. It seemed to enter with great force into every feeling of my heart. I reflected on it again and again, knowing that if any person needed wisdom from God, I did; for how to act I did not know, and unless I could get more wisdom than I then had, would never know; for the teachers of religion of the different sects understood the same passage so differently as to destroy all confidence in settling the question by an appeal to the Bible. At length I came to the conclusion that I must either remain in darkness and confusion, or else I must do as James directs, that is, ask of God. I at length came to the determination to ask of God, concluding that if He gave wisdom to them that lacked wisdom, and would give liberally and not upbraid, I might venture. So, in accordance with this, my determination to ask of God, I retired to the woods to make the attempt. It was on the morning of a beautiful, clear day, early in the spring of eighteen hundred and twenty. It was the first time in my life that I had made such an attempt, for amidst all my anxieties I had never as yet made the attempt to pray vocally.

"After I had retired into the place where I had previously designed to go, having looked around me and finding myself alone, I kneeled down and began to offer up the desires of my heart to God. I had scarcely done so, when immediately I was seized upon by some power which entirely overcame me, and had such astonishing influence over me as to bind my tongue so that I could not speak. Thick darkness gathered around me, and it seemed to me for a time as if I were doomed to sudden destruction. But exerting all my powers to call upon God to deliver me out of the power of this enemy which had seized upon me, and at the very moment when I was ready to sink into despair and abandon myself to destruction, not to an imaginary ruin, but to the power of some actual being from the unseen world, who had such a marvelous power as I had never before felt in any being. Just at this moment of great alarm, I saw a pillar of light exactly over my head above the brightness of the sun, which descended gradually until it fell upon me. It no sooner appeared than I found myself delivered from the enemy which held me bound. When the light rested upon me, I saw two personages, whose brightness and glory defy all description, standing above me in the air. One of them spake unto me, calling me by name, and said (pointing to the other), ' THIS IS MY BELOVED SON, HEAR HIM.'

" My object in going to enquire of the Lord, was to know which of all the sects was right, that I might know which to join. No sooner, therefore, did I get possession of myself, so as to be able to speak, than I asked the personages who stood above me in the light, which of all the sects was right (for at this time it had never entered into my heart that all were wrong), and which I should join. I was answered that I must join none of them, for they were all wrong, and the personage who addressed me said that all their creeds were an abomination in his sight ; that those professors were all corrupt. They draw near to me with their lips, but their hearts are far from me ; they teach for doctrine the commandments of men, having a form of godliness, but they deny the power thereof.

" He again forbade me to join with any of them ; and many other things did he say unto me which I cannot write at this time. When I came to myself again, I found myself lying on my back, looking up into heaven.

" Some few days after I had this vision, I happened to be in company with one of the Methodist preachers who was very active in the before mentioned religious excitement, and conversing with him on the subject of religion, I took occasion to give him an account of the vision which I had had. I was greatly surprised at his behavior ; he treated my communication not only lightly, but with great contempt, saying it was all of the devil, that there were no such things as visions or revelations in these days ; that all such things had ceased with the apostles, and that there never would be any more of them.

" I soon found, however, that my telling the story had excited a great deal of prejudice against me among professors of religion, and was the cause of great persecution, which continued to increase ; and though I was an obscure boy, only between fourteen and fifteen years of age, and my circumstances in life such as to make a boy of no consequence in the world, yet men of high standing would take notice sufficient to excite the public mind against me, and create a hot persecution, and this was common among all sects ; all united to persecute me.

" It has often caused me serious reflection, both then and since, how very strange it was that an obscure boy of a little over fourteen years of age, and one, too, who was doomed to the necessity of obtaining a scanty maintenance by his daily labor, should be thought a character of sufficient importance to attract the attention of the great ones of the most popular sects of the day, so as to create in them a spirit of the hottest persecution and reviling. But strange or not, so it was, and was often a cause of great sorrow to myself. However it was nevertheless, a fact that I had had a vision. I have thought since, that I felt much like Paul when he made his defense before King Agrippa, and related the account of the vision he had when he saw a light and heard a voice, but still there were but few who believed him ; some said he was dishonest, others said he was mad, and he was ridiculed and reviled : but all this did not destroy the reality of his vision. He had seen a vision, he knew he had, and all the persecution under heaven could not make it otherwise ; and though they should persecute him unto death, yet he knew and would know unto his latest breath that he had both seen a light and heard a voice speaking to him, and all the world could not make him think or believe otherwise.

" So it was with me; I had actually seen a light, and in the midst of that light I saw two personages, and they did in reality speak unto me, or one of them did; and though I was

hated and persecuted for saying that I had seen a vision, yet
it was true; and while they were persecuting me, reviling me
and speaking all manner of evil against me, falsely, for so
saying, I was led to say in my heart, Why persecute for
telling the truth? I have actually seen a vision, and who am
I that I can withstand God? Or why does the world think to
make me deny what I have actually seen? For I had seen a
vision. I knew it, and I knew that God knew it, and I could
not deny it, neither dare I do it; at least I knew that by so
doing I would offend God and come under condemnation.

"I had now got my mind satisfied so far as the sectarian
world was concerned, that it was not my duty to join with
any of them, but continue as I was until further directed; I
had found the testimony of James to be true, that a man who
lacked wisdom might ask of God, and obtain and not be
upbraided. I continued to pursue my common avocations in
life until the twenty-first of September, one thousand eight
hundred and twenty-three, all the time suffering severe
persecution at the hands of all classes of men, both religious
and irreligious, because I continued to affirm that I had seen a
vision.

"During the space of time which intervened between the
time I had the vision, and the year eighteen hundred and
twenty-three (having been forbidden to join any of the
religious sects of the day, and being of very tender years, and
persecuted by those who ought to have been my friends, and
to have treated me kindly, and if they supposed me to be
deluded to have endeavored, in a proper and affectionate
manner, to have reclaimed me), I was left to all kinds of
temptations, and mingling with all kinds of society, I
frequently fell into many foolish errors, and displayed the
weakness of youth, and the corruption of human nature,
which I am sorry to say led me into divers temptations, to
the gratification of many appetites offensive in the sight of

God. In consequence of these things I often felt condemned for my weakness and imperfections; when on the evening of the above mentioned twenty-first of September, after I had retired to my bed for the night, I betook myself to prayer and supplication to Almighty God, for forgiveness of all my sins and follies, and also for a manifestation to me, that I might know of my state and standing before him; for I had full confidence in obtaining a divine manifestation, as I had previously had one.

"While I was thus in the act of calling upon God, I discovered a light appearing in the room, which continued to increase until the room was lighter than at noonday, when immediately a personage appeared at my bedside, standing in the air, for his feet did not touch the floor. He had on a loose robe of most exquisite whiteness. It was a whiteness beyond anything earthly I had ever seen; nor do I believe that any earthly thing could be made to appear so exceedingly white and brilliant; his hands were naked, and his arms also, a little above the wrist; so also were his feet naked, as were his legs, a little above the ankles. His head and neck were also bare. I could discover that he had no other clothing on but this robe, as it was open, so that I could see into his bosom.

"Not only was his robe exceedingly white, but his whole person was glorious beyond description, and his countenance truly like lightning. The room was exceedingly light, but not so very bright as immediately around his person. When I first looked upon him I was afraid, but the fear soon left me. He called me by name and said unto me that he was a messenger sent from the presence of God to me, and that his name was Moroni. That God had a work for me to do, and that my name should be had for good and evil among all nations, kindreds, and tongues; or that it should be both good and evil spoken of among all people. He said there was

9

a book deposited, written upon gold plates, giving an account of the former inhabitants of this continent, and the source from whence they sprang.   He also said that the fullness of the everlasting Gospel was contained in it, as delivered by the Savior to the ancient inhabitants.   Also that there were two stones in silver bows (and these stones, fastened to a breast-plate, constituted what is called the Urim and Thummim,) deposited with the plates, and the possession and use of these stones was what constituted Seers in ancient or former times, and that God had prepared them for the purpose of translat-ing the book.

"After telling me these things, he commenced quoting the prophecies of the Old Testament. He first quoted part of the third chapter of Malachi, and he quoted also the fourth or last chapter of the same prophecy, though with a little varia-tion from the way it reads in our Bibles.   Instead of quoting the first verse as it reads in our books, he quoted it thus: 'For behold, the day cometh that shall burn as an oven, and all the proud, yea, and all that do wickedly, shall burn as stub-ble, for they that come shall burn them, saith the Lord of Hosts, that it shall leave them neither root nor branch.' And again, he quoted the fifth verse thus : 'Behold I will reveal unto you the priesthood by the hand of Elijah the prophet, before the coming of the great and dreadful day of the Lord.' He also quoted the next verse differently : 'And he shall plant in the hearts of the children, the promises made to the fathers, and the of hearts the children shall turn to their fathers ; if it were not so, the whole earth would be utterly wasted at His coming.'

"In addition to these, he quoted the eleventh chapter of Isaiah, saying that it was about to be fulfilled. He quoted also the third chapter of Acts, twenty-second and twenty-third verses, precisely as they stand in our New Testament. He said that prophet was Christ, but the day had not yet come when they who would not hear His voice should be cut off from among the people, but soon would come.

"He also quoted the second chapter of Joel, from the twenty-eighth to the last verse. He also said that this was not yet fulfilled, but was soon to be. And he further stated, the fullness of the Gentiles was soon to come in. He quoted many other passages of scripture, and offered many explanations which cannot be mentioned here. Again, he told me that when I got those plates of which he had spoken (for the time that they should be obtained was not yet fulfilled) I should not show them to any person, neither the breastplate with the Urim and Thummim, only to those to whom I should be commanded to show them ; if I did I should be destroyed. While he was conversing with me about the plates, the vision was opened to my mind that I could see the place where the plates were deposited, and that so clearly and distinctly, that I knew the place again when I visited it.

"After this communication, I saw the light in the room begin to gather immediately around the person of him who had been speaking to me, and it continued to do so, until the room was again left dark, except just around him, when instantly I saw, as it were, a conduit open right up into heaven, and he ascended up till he entirely disappeared, and the room was left as it had been before this heavenly light had made its appearance.

"I lay musing on the singularity of the scene, and marveling greatly at what had been told me by this extraordinary messenger, when, in the midst of my meditation, I suddenly discovered that my room was again beginning to get lighted, and in an instant, as it were, the same heavenly messenger was again by my bedside. He commenced, and again related the very same things which he had done at his first visit, without the least variation, which having done, he informed me of great judgments which were coming upon the earth, with great desolations by famine, sword, and pestilence, and that these grievous judgments would come on the earth in this generation. Having related these things, he again ascended as he had done before.

"By this time, so deep were the impressions made on my mind, that sleep had fled from my eyes, and I lay overwhelmed in astonishment at what I had both seen and heard; but what was my surprise when again I beheld the same messenger at my bedside, and heard him rehearse or repeat over again to me the same things as before, and added a caution to me, telling me that Satan would try to tempt me (in consequence of the indigent circumstances of my father's family) to get the plates for the purpose of getting rich. This he forbade me, saying that I must have no other object in view in getting the plates but to glorify God, and must not be influenced by any other motive but that of building his kingdom, otherwise I could not get them. After this third visit, he again ascended up into heaven as before, and I was again left to ponder on the strangeness of what I had just experienced, when almost immediately after the heavenly messenger had ascended from me the third time, the cock crew, and I found that day was approaching, so that our interviews must have occupied the whole of that night. I shortly after arose from my bed, and, as usual, went to the necessary labors of the day, but, in attempting to labor as at other times, I found my strength so exhausted as rendered me entirely unable. My father, who was laboring along with me, discovered something to be wrong with me, and told me to go home. I started with the intention of going to the house, but, in attempting to cross the fence out of the field where we were, my strength entirely failed me, and I fell helpless on the ground, and for a time was quite unconscious of anything. The first thing that I can recollect, was a voice speaking unto me, calling me by name; I looked up and beheld the same messenger standing over my head, surrounded by light, as before. He then again related unto me all that he had related to me the previous night, and commanded me to go to my father, and tell him of the vision and commandment which I had received.

"I obeyed, I returned back to my father in the field and rehearsed the whole matter to him. He replied to me that it was of God, and to go and do as commanded by the messenger. I left the field and went to the place where the messenger had told me the plates were deposited, and owing to the distinctness of the vision which I had had concerning it, I knew the place the instant that I arrived there. Convenient to the village of Manchester, Ontario County, New York, stands a hill of considerable size, and the most elevated of any in the neighborhood. On the west side of this hill, not far from the top, under a stone of considerable size, lay the plates, deposited in a stone box; this stone was thick and rounding in the middle on the upper side, and thinner towards the edges, so that the middle part of it was visible above the ground, but the edge all round was covered with earth. Having removed the earth and obtained a lever, which I got fixed under the edge of the stone, and with a little exertion raised it up; I looked in, and there indeed did I behold the plates, the Urim and Thummim, and the breastplate as stated by the messenger. The box in which they lay was formed by laying stones together in some kind of cement. In the bottom of the box were laid two stones crossways of the box, and on these stones lay the plates and the other things with them. I made an attempt to take them out, but was forbidden by the messenger, and was again informed that the time for bringing them forth had not yet arrived, neither would arrive until four years from that time; but he told me that I should come to that place precisely in one year from that time, and that he would there meet with me, and that I should continue to do so, until the time should come for obtaining the plates.

"Accordingly as I had been commanded, I went at the end of each year, and at each time I found the same messenger there, and received instruction and intelligence from him at each of our interviews, respecting what the Lord was going to do, and how and in what manner his kingdom was to be conducted in the last days.

"As my father's worldly circumstances were very limited, we were under the necessity of laboring with our hands, hiring by day's work and otherwise as we could get opportunity; sometimes we were at home and sometimes abroad, and by continued labor were enabled to get a comfortable maintenance.

"In the year 1824, my father's family met with a great affliction, by the death of my eldest brother, Alvin. In the month of October, 1825, I hired with an old gentleman, by the name of Josiah Stoal, who lived in Chenango County, State of New York. He had heard something of a silver mine having been opened by the Spaniards, in Harmony, Susquehanna County, State of Pennsylvania, and had, previous to my hiring with him, been digging, in order, if possible, to discover the mine. After I went to live with him he took me among the rest of his hands to dig for the silver mine, at which I continued to work for nearly a month without success in our undertaking, and finally I prevailed with the old gentleman to cease digging after it. Hence arose the very prevalent story of my having been a money digger.

"During the time that I was thus employed, I was put to board with a Mr. Isaac Hale, of that place ; it was there that I first saw my wife (his daughter) Emma Hale. On the 18th of January, 1827, we were married, while yet I was employed in the service of Mr. Stoal.

"Owing to my still continuing to assert that I had seen a vision, persecution still followed me, and my wife's father's family were very much opposed to our being married. I was therefore under the necessity of taking her elsewhere, so we went and were married at the house of Squire Tarbill, in South Bainbridge, Chenango County, New York. Immediately after my marriage, I left Mr. Stoal's and went to my father's and farmed with him that season.

" At length the time arrived for obtaining the plates, the Urim and Thummim, and the Breastplate. On the 22nd day of September, 1827, having gone, as usual, at the end of another year, to the place where they were deposited, the same heavenly messenger delivered them up to me with this charge, that I should be responsible for them; that if I should let them go carelessly or through any neglect of mine, I should be cut off; but that if I would use all my endeavors to preserve them, until he, the messenger, should call for them, they should be protected.

"I soon found out the reason why I had received such strict charges to keep them safe, and why it was that the messenger had said, that when I had done what was required at my hand, he would call for them; for no sooner was it known that I had them, than the most strenuous exertions were used to get them from me; every stratagem that could be invented was resorted to for that purpose; the persecution became more bitter and severe than before, and multitudes were on the alert continually to get them from me if possible; but, by the wisdom of God, they remained safe in my hands, until I had accomplished by them what was required at my hand; when according to arrangements, the messenger called for them, I delivered them up to him, and he has them in his charge until this day, being the 2nd of May, 1838.

"The excitement, however, still continued, and rumor, with her thousand tongues, was all the time employed in circulating many tales about my father's family and about myself. If I were to relate a thousandth part of them, it would fill up volumes. The persecution, however, became so intolerable that I was under the necessity of leaving Manchester, and going with my wife to Susquehanna County, in the State of Pennsylvania ; while preparing to start (being very poor, and the persecution so heavy upon us, that there was no probability that we would ever be otherwise), in the midst of our afflictions we found a friend in a gentleman by the name of Martin Harris, who came to us and gave me fifty dollars to assist us in our afflictions. Mr. Harris was a resident of Palmyra Township, Wayne County, in the State of New York, and a farmer of respectability. By this timely aid was I enabled to reach the place of my destination in Pennsylvania, and immediately after my arrival there I commenced copying the characters of the plates. I copied a considerable number of them, and by means of the Urim and Thummim I translated some of them, which I did between the time I arrived at the house of my wife's father in the month of December, and the February following.

"Some time in this month of February, the aforementioned Mr. Martin Harris came to our place, got the characters which I had drawn off the plates, and started with them to the city of New York. For what took place relative to him and the characters, I refer to his own account of the circumstances as he related them to me after his return, which was as follows—

"'I went to the city of New York, and presented the characters which had been translated, with the translation thereof, to Professor Anthon, a gentleman celebrated for his literary attainments. Professor Anthon stated that the translation was correct, more so than any he had before seen translated from the Egyptian. I then showed him those which were not yet translated, and he said that they were Egyptian, Chaldaic, Assyric, and Arabic, and he said that they were the true characters. He gave me a certificate certifying to the people of Palmyra that they were true •

characters, and that the translation of such of them as had been translated was also correct. I took the certificate and put it into my pocket, and was just leaving the house, when Mr. Anthon called me back, and asked me how the young man found out that there were gold plates in the place where he found them. I answered that an angel of God had revealed it to him.

"'He then said unto me, 'Let me see that certificate.' I accordingly took it out of my pocket and gave it to him, when he took it and tore it to pieces. saying that there was no such thing now as ministering of angels, and that if I would bring the plates to him, he would translate them. I informed him that part of the plates were sealed, and that I was forbidden to bring them; he replied, 'I cannot read a sealed book.' I left him and went to Dr. Mitchell, who sanctioned what Professor Anthon had said respecting both the characters and the translation.'

" On the 15th day of April, 1829, Oliver Cowdery came to my house, until when I had never seen him. He stated to me that having been teaching school in the neighborhood where my father resided, and my father being one of those who sent to the school, he went to board for a season at his house, and while there, the family related to him the circumstances of my having the plates, and accordingly he had come to make inquiries of me.

"Two days after the arrival of Mr. Cowdery, (being the 17th of April,) I commenced to translate the Book of Mormon, and he commenced to write for me.

" We still continued the work of translation, when, in the ensuing month, (May, 1829,) we on a certain day went into the woods to pray and inquire of the Lord respecting baptism for the remission of sins, as we found mentioned in the translation of the plates. While we were thus employed, praying and calling upon the Lord, a messenger from heaven descended in a cloud of light, and having laid his hands upon us, he ordained us, saying unto us, '*Upon you, my fellow-servants, in the name of Messiah, I confer the Priesthood of Aaron, which holds the keys of the ministering of angels, and of the gospel of repentance, and of baptism by immersion for the remission of sins; and this shall never be taken again from the earth, until the sons of Levi do offer again an offering unto the Lord in righteousness.*' He said this Aaronic Priesthood had not the power of laying on of hands for the gift of the Holy Ghost, but that this should be conferred on us hereafter; and he commanded us to go and be baptized, and gave us directions that I should baptize Oliver Cowdery, and afterwards that he should baptize me.

"Accordingly we went and were baptized—I baptized him first, and afterwards he baptized me—after which I laid my hands upon his head and ordained him to the Aaronic Priesthood, and afterwards he laid his hands on me and ordained me to the same Priesthood—for so we were commanded.

"The messenger who visited us on this occasion, and conferred this Priesthood upon us, said his name was John, the same that is called John the Baptist in the New Testament, and that he acted under the direction of Peter, James, and John, who held the keys of the Priesthood of Melchisedec, which Priesthood, he said, should in due time be conferred on us, and that I should be called the first elder and he the second. It was on the 15th day of May, 1829, that we were baptized and ordained under the hand of the messenger.

"Immediately upon our coming up out of the water, after we had been baptized, we experienced great and glorious blessings from our Heavenly Father. No sooner had I baptized Oliver Cowdery than the Holy Ghost fell upon him, and he stood up and prophesied many things which would shortly come to pass. And again, so soon as I had been baptized by him, I also had the spirit of prophecy, when, standing up, I prophesied concerning the rise of the Church, and many other things connected with the Church and this generation of the children of men. We were filled with the Holy Ghost, and rejoiced in the God of our salvation.

"Our minds being now enlightened, we began to have the scriptures laid open to our understandings, and the true meaning of their more mysterious passages revealed unto us in a manner which we never could attain to previously, nor ever before had thought of. In the meantime we were forced to keep secret the circumstances of our having been baptized and having received the Priesthood, owing to a spirit of persecution which had already manifested itself in the neighborhood. We. had been threatened with being mobbed, from time to time, and this, too, by professors of religion. And their intentions of mobbing us were only counteracted by the influence of my wife's father's family (under Divine Providence,) who had become very friendly to me, and who were opposed to mobs, and were willing that I should be allowed to continue the work of translation without interruption; and therefore offered and promised us protection from all unlawful proceedings as far as in them lay."

"Have you any further proofs to offer respecting the divine authenticity of this book you refer to?"

"Yes, we have evidence sufficient to establish its divinity beyond doubt, before any impartial court on earth. I will read you from one of our books the voluntary testimony of witnesses who have not been impeached, as follows :

THE TESTIMONY OF THREE WITNESSES.

" Be it known unto all nations, kindreds, tongues, and people unto whom this work shall come, that we, through the grace of God the Father, and our Lord Jesus Christ, have seen the plates which contain this record, which is a record of the people of Nephi, and also of the Lamanites, their brethren, and also of the people of Jared, who came from the tower of which hath been spoken; and we also know that they have been translated by the gift and power of God, for his voice hath declared it unto us; wherefore we know of a surety that the work is true. And we also testify that we have seen the engravings which are upon the plates; and they have been shewn unto us by the power of God, and not of man. And we declare with words of soberness, that an angel of God came down from heaven, and he brought and laid before our eyes, that we beheld and saw the plates, and the engravings thereon; and we know that it is by the grace of God the Father, and our Lord Jesus Christ, that we beheld and bear record that these things are true; and it is marvellous in our eyes, nevertheless the voice of the Lord commanded us that we should bear record of it; wherefore, to be obedient unto the commandments of God, we bear testimony of these things. And we know that if we are faithful in Christ, we shall rid our garments of the blood of all men, and be found spotless before the judgment-seat of Christ, and shall dwell with him eternally in the heavens. And the honor be to the Father, and to the Son, and to the Holy Ghost, which is one God. Amen.

OLIVER COWDERY,
DAVID WHITMER,
MARTIN HARRIS.

" Can you give us any other evidences respecting this record?"

"Yes, here is also the testimony of eight additional witnesses, who declare they saw the plates."

AND ALSO THE TESTIMONY OF EIGHT WITNESSES.

"Be it known unto all nations, kindreds, tongues, and people unto whom this work shall come, that Joseph Smith, Jun., the translator of this work, has shown unto us the plates of which hath been spoken, which have the appearance of gold; and as many of the leaves as the said Smith has translated, we did handle with our hands; and we also saw the engravings thereon, all of which has the appearance of ancient work, and of curious workmanship. And this we bear record with words of soberness, that the said Smith has shown unto us, for we have seen and hefted, and know of a surety that the said Smith has got the plates of which we have spoken. And we give our names unto the world, to witness unto the world that which we have seen; and we lie not, God bearing witness of it.

CHRISTIAN WHITMER,	HIRAM PAGE,
JACOB WHITMER,	JOSEPH SMITH, SEN.,
PETER WHITMER, JUN.,	HYRUM SMITH,
JOHN WHITMER,	SAMUEL H. SMITH.

"There is one point," said Brown, "upon which I would like to hear further: it is the restoration, before mentioned. If these things are true, then the gospel was not upon the earth at the time of Joseph Smith's birth, and, as you will admit, the Church was organized in the days of Christ and left on the earth when He ascended on high: the question then arises, how the Gospel was it taken from the earth?"

"Let me give you another quotation from the Bible on the subject," said the Elder. "'From the days of John the Baptist until now the kingdom of heaven suffereth violence ; and the violent take it by force.' (Matthew xi: 12.) By parity of reasoning where would our own government be if subjected to similar treatment? Suppose, that instead of Christ being crucified, it were the President, that the Cabinet instead of the Apostles were murdered, the Congress and not the Seventies were scattered to the four winds, and our citizens were subjected to the fate of the Saints of old in being driven beneath the earth—what would then remain of our nation? It exists now proudly and gloriously, and has existed for more than a century, but such treatment would leave it to future generations as only an incident in history—that is, it came, it flourished and it passed away, just as did the true religion in the early days; and it might again, also like the true religion, be restored, even as the Roman Empire rose, fell and rose again."

"I understand."

"If you have no objections, I would like to read to you the words of a wise man on this subject, which will illustrate my meaning in a much clearer way than it is possible for me to express it myself. The quotation is not long and you will all—especially my legal friend—see the force of his argument. He uses these words :

"'Now, in order to come at this subject in plainness, let us examine the constitution of earthly governments in regard to the authority and laws of adoption. We will say, for instance, the President of the United States writes a commission to A. B., duly authorizing him to act in some office in the government, and during his administration, two gentlemen from Europe come to reside in this country, and being strangers and foreigners wishing to become citizens, they go before A. B., and he administers

the oath of allegiance in due form, and certifies
the same, and this constitutes them legal citizens, entitled to the privileges of those who are
citizens or subjects by birth. After these things
A. B. is taken away by death, and C. D., in
looking over his papers happens to find the
commission given to A. B., and applying it to his
own use, assumes the vacant office; meantime,
two foreigners arrive and apply for citizenship,
and being informed by persons ignorant of the
affairs of government that C. D. could administer the laws of adoption, they submit to be administered unto by C. D., without once exam-
ining his authority; C. D. certifies of their
citizenship, and they suppose they have been
legally adopted, the same as the others, and are
entitled to the privileges of citizenship. But,
by and by, their citizenship is called into question, and they produce the certificates of C. D.;
the President inquires, 'Who is C. D.? I never
gave him a commission to act in any office, I
know him not and you are strangers and

foreigners to the commonwealth, until you go
before the legally appointed successor of A. B.,
or some other of like authority, who has a commission from the President direct in his own
name.' . In the meantime C. D. is taken and
punished according to law, for practicing im-
position, and usurping authority which was
never conferred upon him. And so it is with
the kingdom of God. The Lord authorized the
Apostles and others, by direct revelation, and
by the spirit of prophecy, to preach and baptize, and build up His church and kingdom ;
but after awhile they died, and a long time
passed away; men reading over their commission, where it says to the eleven Apostles,
'Go ye into all the world and preach the gospel
to every creature,' etc., have had the presump-
tion to apply these sayings as their authority,
and, without any other commission, have gone
forth professing to preach the gospel, and baptize, and build up the church and kingdom. of
God ; but those whom they baptize never receive

10

the same blessings and gifts which character-
ized a Saint, or citizen of the kingdom, in the
days of the Apostles. Why? Because they
are yet foreigners and strangers, for the commission given to the Apostles never commissioned any other man to act in their stead.
This was a prerogative the Lord preserved unto
Himself. No man has a right to take this ministry upon himself, but he that is called by revelation, and duly qualified to act in his calling
by the Holy Ghost."

"You give us abundance of authority, as well
as your own testimony and evidence," said the
doctor. "You have developed a wide and pro-
found subject for our consideration, and for one
I regret that we cannot at once hear you out,
that is, go to the end of the subject with you,
and know all that you are in possession of in
regard to it. Right or wrong, one thing is
plainly manifest—that you convey a philosophy
each part of which is so reasonable, consistent
and harmonious with every other part, and with

the ground-work itself, that he who doubts must question himself as to why he doubts. And now, let me ask, will it not be practicable for you to remain another day?"

"While it would give me, personally, the greatest pleasure to do so, it must be remembered that I am not performing this work for my own individual gratification. The field is a broad one, and just think how small a portion of it I would be able to cover should I give way to my present inclinations and remain unduly long in places where everything is so pleasant as here. No, I must go, but hope to return to this region again."

"Well, of course you understand your own affairs best, but you are making such headway here that I hoped it might be desirable for you to continue to the end."

"So it would but for the reasons stated. My train departs at 11 o'clock tomorrow, and I must fill the appointments I have made."

CHAPTER IX.

THAT MORMON AGAIN.

SOME months had passed away since the Elder took his departure from Westminster, and during this time his name had been on everybody's lips, both for good and evil. The principles advanced by him had taken such root in the minds of many that it seemed impossible for them to lay the doctrine aside. Among this class were the Marshalls, who, by the way, had increased their family by the addition of a son-in-law, their daughter Claire having, as was anticipated, changed her name from Marshall to Sutherland.

Herbert Sutherland was a rising young man of Westminster, well and favorably known to most of the people. He had for several years been very much attached to Miss Marshall, and, as the love was mutual, of course no one appeared surprised in the least when the wedding took place. Joy, and promise of an unclouded life, seemed to be the portion of the young couple.

Breakfast had been waiting for over an hour for Mr. Marshall, and his good wife had become almost impatient when the gate opened and he entered, saying to his wife, "You must overlook this delay, as I have been detained at the station. While passing, I noticed a familiar friend and could not resist the temptation of spending with him the forty minutes given for transferring baggage, even when aware that the detention kept you and the breakfast waiting."

"Well I declare," said Mrs. Marshall, "you must have met a very esteemed friend indeed, to have remained so long at the expense of so many."

"Who was it, papa?" remarked Claire; "it's no use asking us to guess, for you know we are not Yankees enough for that."

"One would imagine you had been in the presence of a number of friends," said Mr. Sutherland, "judging from the pleased expression on your face."

"Well, why not tell us who it was?" said Mrs. Marshall.

"It was one whose visit with us was very short, but whose name has been mentioned since scores of times," Mr. Marshall answered; "and now we will go to the dining room, and, in the meantime, I will tell you what my conversation was with Mr. Charles Durant, of Salt Lake City, our Mormon friend.

"I had learned that he promised while here to visit you again," remarked Mr. Sutherland, "and is it possible, he has been so near and yet failed to keep his promise? I did not think this of Mr. Durant, for, while I have not had the pleasure of his acquaintance, I had formed a very good opinion of him from remarks made by others, and was in hopes of seeing him myself some day."

"And so you shall," answered Mr. Marshall,
"I tell you he has not forgotten. He is on his
way home, it is true, but has taken a trip up the
country for a few days, and intends visiting us
when he returns."

"That's better," said Sutherland; "I do not
wish to miss what you people claimed was a
treat to you."

With this the family adjourned to the dining
room, where Mr. Marshall acquainted them with
all the facts received from Mr. Durant. He had
performed his work to the entire satisfaction of
the president of the Southern States Mission,
and had been given a leave of absence to return
home; but he had received word while *en route*
that some Elders had been terribly beaten by
a band of fanatics. He was instructed to pay
his fellow laborers a visit, and administer to
their wants before continuing his homeward
journey. While he had in view a pleasant visit
with the Marshalls, he could not think of enjoying the same before performing a duty to the

brethren in distress. He would be with the Marshalls in a day or two and would then remain some days in their company.

"He has promised," said Mr. Marshall, "to answer all the questions we have been accumulating for him, and will be pleased indeed to have as many of our neighbors spend the evening with him as we are willing to invite."

"Exactly what Herbert has been wishing for," exclaimed Claire, "knowing so well that Mr. Durant and the Mormon gospel doctrines have made a deep impression on us, he has been very anxious to converse with this missionary."

"Yes," answered Sutherland, "if all I have heard from you is correct, then I am surprised that this peculiar people are despised to such an extent. The principles you have explained to me, as received from him, are logical and good, and Mr. Brown tells me they have had such an influence with him, that nothing short of a visit to Salt Lake City will satisfy the longing

he has to study the Mormon question as he
desires; and as for Claire, why she has gone
over her Bible and marked the passages quoted
by the Elder, until the Sacred Book looks like a
Chinese record."

"And better than that," exclaimed his young
wife, "I have committed the most of them to
memory, and should he desire an assistant, I
can surprise not only him but all of you with
my knowledge of those principles. I realize
how much happiness God has given me in this
world, and how much I should endeavor to
please Him, and have therefore devoted more
time to reading His word than ever before, and,
strange to say, I have found passages quoted by
Mr. Durant whenever I have read, and the
verses marked in my Bible seem to lead to something else that he has said. His testimony is
so deeply rooted in my heart that I almost
believe his people will yet be my people, and
his faith will be my faith."

"Why, Claire," said her mother, "if you are

not careful, you will be a Mormon before you are aware."

" And should you become one," said her husband, "think of your many friends, and the opinions they will have of you."

" Well, I haven't joined the Mormons yet," said Claire; " but if I do, it will be because I believe them to be right; and if I have your good will, Herbert, and that of papa and mamma, what care I for the opinions of others?"

" Well said," answered Herbert, with a smile; " but we will see if we cannot 'corner' your missionary, get him into an argumentative jail, if you please, from which it will be difficult or impossible for him to escape. Should he be able to make the gospel he teaches as plain and as reasonable as the doctrines that are set forth in the tracts which he left here, I can see no reason why any earnest, sincere searcher after knowledge cannot adopt that gospel as a living truth."

It was agreed, thereupon, that when the

promised telegram from Durant should be received, giving the date of his arrival, the neighbors were to be invited, and the large dining room wonld be turned into an informal meeting place where the principles of the gospel, as believed in by the Mormons, could be further explained. This was accordingly done.

CHAPTER X.

THE MISSIONARY'S RETURN.

ELDER CHARLES DURANT returned to Westminster just ten days after the time of his meeting with Mr. Marshall, at the station. He was heartily welcomed by the family, and being comfortably seated at the dinner table, the conversation naturally drifted to a detailed account of his experience since his first visit. His labors had been divided somewhat in two or three different states. He had met with many kinds of people, and with a variety of treatments, since leaving the home of the Marshalls; he made many friends as well as a few enemies, but had endeavored to perform his work in a way to meet the approbation of that Being who had commissioned him to spread His word among the children of men. Having performed his work to the satisfaction of those under whom he labored, he was, as previously stated, released therefrom, for a time at least, and had commenced his journey towards the land of his birth, where dwelt his loved ones, when the telegram reached him from the president of the Mission to the effect that several Elders had been mobbed in a neighboring county, and asking that he visit his brethren on his way home, as stated before.

After the meal, the family adjourned to the sitting room when the missionary was requested to give an account of the mobbing of the Elders whom he had just visited.

He said that they had been laboring for several months holding meetings wherever they could get an opportunity, and had succeeded in obtaining the permission of the trustees to hold their meetings in a schoolhouse—they being solicited to hold religious services by the people, and explain the gospel to them.

A family named Brooks expressed a desire to be baptized, and the Elders had consented to

perform the ordinance on a fixed day, according
to their custom, and in conformity with the plan
of salvation as pointed out by Christ, the early
Apostles, and by John the Baptist who baptized
openly in the river Jordan, and near "Ænon
near to Salim because there was much water
there."

At the appointed time the ordinance was performed, a number of persons being present who
came for the purpose of sneering at the rite, and
making sport of its sacredness, which they did,
but which the Elders paid only little attention
to, being accustomed to the jeers of the wicked.
On the same evening there was a pleasant asso-
ciation at the residence of the newly-baptized
family, the time being spent in singing sacred
songs, and in conversation. Retiring at 9
o'clock, leaving their bedroom door open owing
to the heat, they were at 11 o'clock rudely
awakened, ordered to get up, to accompany a
mob of about fifteen men to the woods.

"You are a pretty-looking lot of fellows,"

said one of the Elders as he counted them, and glanced at their masked faces.

"What do you consider the Savior would think of your mission, if He were here? Why do you disturb the slumbers of the peaceful citizens at night, thus hideously masked? If we have transgressed any law, we are amenable; take us before your magistrates, and we will answer to any charge you may prefer."

"We don't want you to preach any more in this locality," said one of the masked men.

"Then the best way to stop us is to induce the people to cease attending our meetings."

At this juncture the inmates of the house were alarmed, and Mr. B. came in, taking a glance at each of the disturbers.

A voice on the outside was heard to cry: "Captain! captain! enough said, enough said."

The mob then withdrew, and the Elders retired again, still leaving the door unlocked. They remained there the following day, but subsequently spent some time visiting friends in

other districts. In the course of two weeks they
returned to the same place. On their way thither,
there were a few who hurled insults at them,
but to this they paid no attention. They arrived at Mr. Brooks' house at 5 o'clock in the
evening where they met companions, and where
the time was spent in speaking of the gospel,
singing hymns, and in conversing upon a variety
of subjects concerning Utah and her people.
No signs of disturbance appeared, save an occa-
sional ominous bark of the house dog.

The Elders retired with sweet recollections of
home, to be roughly awakened at 2 o'clock at
night, by the harsh cry of "Surrender." They
were surrounded by a horde of ruffians, armed
with guns, pistols and clubs; and in the most
blasphemous language, were ordered to get up,
the mobbers in the meantime brandishing their
weapons in the faces of the Elders. Not obeying
orders as rapidly as the mob wished them to,
they were each (there being four of them),
seized by two of the cowards, one on either side,

dragged from their beds in an inhuman manner, and marched along the road, an eighth of a mile, dressed only in their thin summer night-clothing. Resistance was impossible, and the attempt of the proprietor of the house to assist them was met with curses, a blow across the forehead, with the exclamation: "If you show your head out of this house before 6 o'clock tomorrow morning, we will kill you."

The train marched on, the vilest curses and the blackest oaths being uttered against them that mortals can express. There was no charge preferred against them, and they said: "If we have broken any law, take us before the courts," but the only reply was:

"We are law enough for you."

What was to be their fate, they knew not, until the mob began cutting and trimming limbs of trees from four to six feet long, having ugly knots. Soon the Elders were ordered to bend over a fallen log about two feet through, when their doom was made plain to them. They were

11

terribly whipped, receiving lash after lash upon their backs without a question being asked, or an opportunity being afforded to appeal from this inhuman treatment. Occasionally they raise to say a word, but are immediately thrust down again by some of the mob using pistols or clubs. In this way three received severe scalp wounds. The woods resound with the lashes and the groans of the tortured ; thirty-five stripes have been laid upon them, when they are requested to leave the country. Too faint to comply, their hesitancy is construed as a refusal, and they are once more belabored with redoubled fury, causing them to cringe beneath the cruel beech-limbs wielded by a sturdy fiend weighing over two-hundred pounds. Fifty stripes each, they received, and yet they had injured no man ! How terrible ! but it was all for the sake of the gospel. Finally after such torture, they were released, upon promising to leave the country the next day.

They returned to their friend and brother !

but in what a lacerated condition. They found him sitting in the door bleeding from his wounds. They dressed each other's wounds as best they could, then lay down in troubled rest till morning, when they departed to the place where Elder Durant met them, perhaps never to return.

While rehearsing not only his own experience but that of his wounded brothers, no one listened with more marked attention than Claire's husband. From the moment he was introduced to Durant, at the depot, they became very much attached to each other, and, as expressed by Mr. Sutherland, it seemed as if they had always been acquainted.

Later, while these two were conversing upon the veranda, Mr. Sutherland interrupted the Elder by asking : "How do you account for the peculiar feelings attending the formation of new friendship, Mr. Durant ? Have you not noticed that upon many occasions when introduced to a person, you feel as well acquainted as if you had known him for years ?"

"Yes," replied Elder Durant, "I have noticed it often, and have frequently wondered if occasions where such feelings are manifested were really the beginning of acquaintance."

"I have certainly been very much impressed with this sensation at times when I have been absolutely certain of its being the first meeting," replied Sutherland ; "for instance, to be frank, it is the case with you. I am certain beyond question that you and I háve never met previous to this day, and yet I followed you while giving the account of your labors and the troubles of your brethren, with as much interest as if you were my own brother ; and I have felt all day long that we have always been acquainted."

"Mr. Sutherland," said the Elder, "who knows but before now we have been better acquainted than you are with any gentleman in your village, and that we have merely forgotten our former associations together ?"

"I do not understand your meaning," said Sutherland, "I am certain we have never seen each other before, and consequently I cannot comprehend your idea when you intimate that perhaps we have been well acquainted. You came from the West, while I have always lived here, where you have never dwelt except during your former| visit to Mr. Marshall's home, and how, therefore, can it be possible for us ever to have met before?

"I do not claim for an instant that such is the case, Mr. Sutherland, but the idea afforded me such a splendid chance to open a conversation upon a principle believed in by my people, that I could not resist the opportunity of saying what I did, and, as you say you are desirous of learning all you can about our views upon religious principles, you, yourself, gave me a thought, serving as a text, for dwelling upon one of the most important of these."

"If that is the case, I am very glad. What is the principle?"

"You know that all Christians believe that after death there is life?"

"Of course, or why should they take the pains to prepare for death? But what has that to do with having met you before?"

"Neither that nor what I am going to say has anything whatever to do with it, but, Mr. Sutherland, if it is reasonable for you and me to believe we shall live after death, why should it be unreasonable for us also to believe that our spirits existed before the birth of our earthly tabernacles? There is certainly something connected with the intelligence of man that should appeal to us as if to say that the spirit is older than the body, and emanated from a more exalted place than this earth of ours."

"Why, Mr. Durant," exclaimed Sutherland in astonishment, "I never heard such a doctrine as that."

"Let me ask, have you ever read the Bible to any great extent?"

"Yes, I have always been a lover of the Divine Record, and have spent many hours in its perusal."

"I am glad to hear this, and I think, as we proceed, you may change your mind regarding never having heard such a doctrine as pre-existence. You will perhaps admit that while reading, you failed to understand fully what you read. As an introduction to this grand and glorious principle, let me read a beautiful poem I have here from the pen of one of the gifted women of Utah ; she is dead now, and the intelligent spirit, sent from God to dwell in her earthly tabernacle, has been recalled by the Being who sent it, or, as the Bible declares, 'has returned to God who gave it.' Her name was Eliza R. Snow Smith, and that name, as well as this poem, will live while time endures:"

"O my Father, thou that dwellest
In the high and glorious place!
When shall I regain thy presence,
And again behold thy face?
In thy holy habitation,
Did my spirit once reside?
In my first, primeval childhood,
Was I nurtured near thy side?

" For a wise and glorious purpose
Thou hast placed me here on earth,
And withheld the recollection
Of my former friends and birth;
Yet oft-times a secret something
Whispered, You're a stranger here;
And I felt that I had wandered
From a more exalted sphere.

" I had learned to call thee Father,
Through thy Spirit from on high;
But, until the Key of Knowledge
Was restored, I knew not why.
In the heavens are parents single?
No; the thought makes reason stare!
Truth is reason; truth eternal
Tells me, I've a mother there.

" When I leave this frail existence,
   When I lay this mortal by,
   Father, mother, may I meet you
   ⚫ In your royal court on high?
   Then, at length, when I've completed
     All you sent me forth to do,
   With your mutual approbation
     Let me come and dwell with you."

" That is one of the most beautiful composi-
tions I have'ever listened to, Mr. Durant. The
words appear to carry a strange conviction with
them. Can it be true? and if so, are we here as
school children, sent by exalted parents, to become acquainted with sorrow in order to understand happiness? "

"Either this is the case, or else our faith in a
hereafter is a myth. You prove to me that our
birth is the commencement. of the intelligence
of man, and you also convince me that death is
its end. But we have enough given in the
scriptures to convince us that birth is not the
beginning, and likewise that death is not
the end. Christ said He came forth from the

Father (John xvi : 28), and it was His prayer
that the glory which He had before coming
would be His when He returned. (John xvii :
5.) In His teachings to His Apostles He must
have familiarized them with this exalted principle of pre-existence, for upon one occasion
they came to Him with a question, concerning
a blind man : 'Who did sin, this man or his
parents, that he was born blind?' (John ix : 2.)
Surely had this been a foolish question, Christ
would have corrected them, but He answered
them in a manner leading us to understand that
it was a principle firmly believed in by them
all ; and comprehending this, as certainly they
did, they, more than our generation, could intelligently lisp the prayer taught them by the
Master : 'Our Father who art in heaven.'
Our Divine Record says that God is the Father
of the spirits of all flesh (Num. xvi : 22), in
whose hand is the soul of every living thing
(Job xii : 10); and we find in it that when
death comes, the spirit of man will return to

God who gave it. (Eccl. xii: 7.) Job was asked by the Lord where he was when the foundation of the earth was laid (Job. xxxviii: 3–7), and the Almighty declared He not only knew but ordained Jeremiah to be a prophet before his earthly birth. (Jer. i: 5.) From these passages, and many others that might be cited, it should be very easy for Christians to understand that there is a natural and a spiritual body." (I. Cor. xv: 44.)

"Mr. Durant," said Sutherland, "whether this principle is true or otherwise, it cannot be gainsaid that you have scripture to support it."

"Why should we not have, Mr. Sutherland? It is truth, and it is only natural that the truth should appear reasonable. As quoted, God asks Job : 'Who laid the corner stones of this earth, when the morning stars sang together and all the sons of God shouted for joy?' (Job xxxviii: 7.) Now I sincerely believe that we were there, that we helped to compose that large congregation of sons of God, and that we *did* shout for joy at beholding the time approaching when we also would have the privilege of visiting an earth where our Father would give us an opportunity to become possessed of bodies which should eventually be eternal abiding places for our spirits ; that when we came to this school we should have our judgments taken away, or, in other words, that all recollection of our former existence should be withdrawn, in order that we might be able to use the greatest gift of all, which is "free agency," to do good or evil and become to a certain extent Gods in embryo, and then when we returned home from this school our Father could reward us, his children, ac-. cording to our works."

" Your explanation carries with it conviction. I have been very much interested and desire to talk further with you on this subject, but fear I am doing you an injustice by requiring you to speak so much. I must not forget that the neighbors are coming in tonight, and I should therefore not weary you."

"You need not fear, I assure you : I have been talking now upon these principles for two years ; it is my mission, and I am well pleased to find people who are willing to hear."

"I am very anxious to listen, I can assure you," replied Mr. Sutherland. Let us walk through the village, you can view our improvements, and perhaps shake hands with many whom you met when here before ; we might then return in time for supper, and rest awhile before our evening chat."

This proposition was agreed to, and taking their hats, the two men went out. The first person met on the ramble was our medical friend, who, learning of Mr. Durant's intended return, was hastening to the Marshall residence to welcome him. The greeting which the young missionary received from his true and lasting friend was unaffected and sincere, meaning more than language can express. Questions and answers regarding the missionary's trip, and matters, which to the general reader would

amount to mere commonplace, were exchanged
by the conversation, and must have been interesting to them, for it was continued during the
whole of what proved a very long walk.

"I begin to feel quite like a resident here,"
said the Elder, "though, perhaps, I ought to say
that my acquaintance is not the only cause for
that feeling, for I try to be at ease wherever I go."

"And succeed I should say. If your experience elsewhere has been anything like that at
Westminster."

"Yes, indeed, and in so doing I find no little
comfort in the words of an eminent man who is
classed as a 'pagan,' an agnostic, and so on,
but who, I verily believe, was as much a Christian at heart as most of us—certainly much
more so than many who engage in the promulga-
tion of Christianity as a profession: 'The
world is my home, and humanity my kindred.'"

By this time they had reached the home of
Mr. Marshall, and after supper, preparations
were made for the evening gathering.

CHAPTER XI.

A PLEASANT INTERVIEW.

IN the evening Elder Durant not only had the pleasure of meeting all his old friends of the previous visit, but was honored with the presence of a large number of persons whom he had not seen before. Some of them had attended the meeting he held in the Town Hall on his first visit, while others had only heard of him through the Marshalls.

When all were comfortably seated in the large dining room, Mr. Sutherland by way of introducing the missionary to his new friends, said :

" My friends and neighbors, we have assembled here this evening for the purpose of listening to Mr. Durant on the religious faith of a people who claim to have the keys of a new dispensation committed to them. If their

claim is correct, then it is of the utmost importance to the whole human race.   If God has
indeed spoken from the heavens, it is the duty
of His children to listen ; on the other hand, if
this claim of the Mormons be founded on a
myth, then it is our duty to do all in our power
to disprove their declarations, and deny that
they have any divine commission whatever to
proclaim the principles of salvation.   You who
have the privilege of listening to him will
know whether his arguments are sound and
scriptural, or otherwise ; and can therefore exercise the right, which you all have, of judging for
yourselves.   We will, therefore, ask our friend
from the valleys of the West to give us, in as
few words as possible, an outline of what Mormonism teaches, after which all may act with
the utmost freedom in asking questions upon
anything the gentleman may say, or upon any
principle believed in by his people.   Now, Mr.
Durant, we are anxious to hear you, and you will
find us attentive listeners."

The Elder arose and in a few well-chosen words expressed his thanks to the Marshalls for their kindness, as well as to Mr. Sutherland, and all his friends who had taken an interest in him. He was pleased to answer questions pertaining to his faith, and with all sincerity bore testimony that the Mormons were less understood by the people of this and other nations than any other sect in Christendom. Their mission is one of "peace on earth and good will to man," notwithstanding they had been represented as having objects quite the reverse.

Their faith teaches the reason why man is here in this probation ; whence man came, and whither he goes, after his departure by death. It teaches that the destiny of man is mighty, that his exaltation is to be great ; that what man is, God once was ; that what God is, man can be.

"Mormonism teaches men to believe in God, the Eternal Father, and in His Son Jesus Christ, and in the Holy Ghost, who bears record of them forever.

12

"As a people, we believe that all mankind, through the transgression of our first parents, were brought under the curse and penalty for transgression ; but that through the atoning sacrifice, sufferings, and death of Jesus Christ, all are to be redeemed from any effects of original transgression ; that 'as by the offense of one, judgment came upon all men unto condemnation ; even so, by the righteousness of one, the free gift came upon all men unto the justification of life.' (Rom. v : 18.)

"We believe that little children are innocent, and not under transgression ; that they are incapable of obeying any law, not understanding good or evil ; and Jesus says, 'Of such are the kingdom of heaven ;' but then, when they arrive at the years of maturity, and know good from evil, and are capable of obeying or disobeying law ; if they then transgress, they will be condemned for breaking a known law.

"We believe that no man will be condemned for not obeying a law that he does not know ;

and that consequently millions of the human
family who have never heard the gospel, are
more blessed than those who have had that
privilege, and have refused to accept it ; that
mankind will be judged according to the deeds
done in the body.

"We believe in the sufferings, death and
atoning sacrifice of our Lord and Savior Jesus
Christ, and in His resurrection and ascension
on high, and in the Holy Ghost, which is given
to all who obey the gospel.

" We believe, first, it is necessary to have faith
in God, and that, next, it is necessary to repent
of our sins—to confess and to turn away from
them, and make restitution to all whom we have
injured, as far as it is in our power.

"We believe that the third necessity is to be
baptized by immersion in water, in the name of
the Father, Son, and Holy Ghost, 'for remission
of sins,' and that this ordinance must be performed by one having authority, or otherwise
it is of no avail.

"The fourth is, to receive the laying on of
hands, in the name of Jesus Christ, for the gift
of the Holy Ghost ; and this ordinance must also
be administered by the Apostles or the Elders,
whom the Lord Jesus has called to lay on hands,
nor then is it of any advantage except to those
persons who have complied with the before-
named three conditions.

"We believe that the Holy Ghost is the
same now, as it was in the apostolic days, and
that when a church is organized, it is its privilege to have all the gifts, powers and blessings
which flow from the Holy Spirit :

" 'Such, for instance, as the gifts of revelation, prophecy, visions, the ministry of angels,
healing the sick by the laying on of hands in
the name of Jesus, the working of miracles, and,
in short, all the gifts mentioned in the scriptures, or enjoyed by the ancient Saints.' We
believe that inspired apostles and prophets,
together with all the officers as mentioned in

the New Testament, are necessary in the Church
in these days.

"We believe that there has been a general
and awful apostasy from the religion of the
New Testament, so that all the known world
have been left for centuries without the church
of Christ among them ; without a priesthood
authorized of God to administer ordinances ;
that every one of the churches has perverted
the gospel, some in one way and some in another.   For instance, almost every church has
ignored the doctrine of 'immersion for the remission of sins.'   Those few who have practiced
it have abolished the ordinance of the 'laying
on of hands' upon baptized believers for the
gifts of the Holy Ghost. Again the few who
have practiced the last ordinance have perverted
the first, or have denied the ancient gifts,
powers and blessings which flow from the Holy
Spirit, or have said to the inspired apostles and
prophets, we have to need of you in the body.
Those few, again, who have believed in, and con-

tended for, the miraculous gifts and powers of
the Holy Spirit, have perverted the ordinances.
Thus all the churches preach false doctrines
and distort the gospel, and instead of having
authority from God to administer its ordinances,
they are under the curse of God for corrupting
it. Paul says (Gal. i: 8), ' Though we or an
angel from heaven preach any other gospel unto
you than that which we have preached unto you,
let him be accursed.'

"We believe that there are a few sincere,
honest and humble persons who are striving to
do according to the best of their understanding,
but, in many respects, they err in doctrine because of false teachers and the precepts of men,
and that they will receive the fullness of the
gospel with gladness as soon as they hear it."

"We believe in the Bible, Book of Mormon,
and in living and continued revelation ; but we
also believe that no new revelation will contra-
dict the old.

"The gospel in the Book of Mormon is the

same as that in the New Testament, so that no
one who reads it can misunderstand its principles. It has been revealed by the angel to be
preached as a witness to all nations, first to the
Gentiles and then to the Jews, then cometh the
downfall of Babylon. Thus fulfilling the vision
of John, which he beheld on the Isle of Patmos, (Rev. xiv: 6, 7, 8), 'And I saw another
angel fly in the midst of heaven, having the
everlasting gospel to preach unto them that
dwell upon the earth, and to every nation, and
kindred, and tongue, and people, saying with a
loud voice, fear God and give glory to Him, for
the hour of His judgment is come ; and worship Him that made the heaven and earth, and
the sea and the fountains of water.' And there
followed another angel saying, 'Babylon is
fallen, is fallen, that great city, because she
made all nations drink of the wine of the wrath
of her fornications.'

"Many revelations and prophecies have been
given to this Church since its rise, which have

been printed and sent forth to the world. These also contain the gospel in great plainness, and instructions of infinite importance to the Saints. They also unfold the great events that await this generation, the terrible judgments to be poured forth upon the wicked, and the blessings and glories to be given to the righteous. We believe God will continue to give revelations by visions, by the ministry of angels, and by the inspiration of the Holy Ghost, until the Saints are guided into all truth.

" We believe that wherever the people enjoy the religion of the New Testament, there they enjoy visions, revelations, the ministry of angels, etc. And that wherever these blessings cease to be enjoyed, there they also cease to enjoy the religion of the New Testament.

" We believe that God has established His church in order to prepare a people for His second coming in the clouds of heaven, in power and great glory; and that then the Saints that are asleep in their graves will be raised and reign with Him on earth a thousand years.

"We believe that great judgments await the earth on account of the wickedness of its inhabitants, and that when the gospel shall have been sufficiently proclaimed, if they reject it they will be destroyed ; that plagues, pestilence and famine will be multiplied upon them ; that thrones will be cast down, empires overthrown, and nations destroyed ; that when the Spirit of God ceases to restrain the people, the world will be full of blood, carnage and desolation ; that peace will be taken from the earth and from among all people, religious and irreligious. It shall be as with the people, so with the priest, etc.

"We believe that the Lord will gather His people from among all nations unto a land of peace, and give them pastors after His own heart, who shall feed them with knowledge and understanding, and they shall be the only people upon the earth that shall not be at war with one another.

"We believe that the Ten Tribes of Israel, with the dispersed of Judah, shall soon be restored to their own lands, according to the covenants which God made with their ancient fathers, and that when this great work of restitution shall take place, the power of God shall be made manifest in signs, and wonders, and mighty deeds, far exceeding anything that took place in the exodus from Egypt. Jerusalem will be rebuilt, together with the glorious temple, and the Lord shall visit His Saints in Zion. In that day the name of the Lord shall become great unto the ends of the earth, and all nations shall serve and obey Him, for the wicked shall have perished out of the earth. :]

"We believe in all principles of truth that have been revealed ; in all that are now being revealed, and are prepared to receive all that God will reveal.

"We believe that the gospel, now being preached by the Latter-day Saints, is to call the honest in heart out of Babylon, that they partake not of her sins nor receive of her plagues.   .

"We believe in morality, chastity, purity, virtue and honesty, and wish to promote the happiness of our fellow-men."

The Elder's words were listened to with marked attention. He expressed a. willingness to answer questions, and a desire to have as many asked, concerning the religious principles believed in by his people, as the listeners were pleased to propound.

"Mr. Durant," said Sutherland, when the former was seated, "I have not only listened to all you have said with the greatest interest, but have taken pleasure in reading the tracts left while on your former visit, and whether your faith is correct or otherwise, it will be a difficult task to disprove any of your arguments by the Sacred Record. I wish to ask you a few questions regarding some of the principles you have not touched upon, and which I understand to be a part of your faith. I am informed that you believe in a literal resurrection of the body ? Is this correct ?"

" Certainly," answered the Elder promptly. " How could we lay any claim whatever to a Christian belief in the resurrection unless we believed in a literal resurrection ?"

" Well you certainly would not be compelled to believe in a literal resurrection in order to lay claim to having a Christian belief in that principle, for all Christians are surely not believers in it."

" All true Christians must follow Christ's teachings regarding this principle as well as all others, or else how can they be considered true Christians? Christ is the resurrection and the life. (John xi : 25.) He was also the first fruits of the resurrection. (Acts xxvi: 23.) He, therefore, is our great pattern. We know He was put to death (Matt. xxvii: 50); that His body was laid in the tomb (Matt. xxvii: 60); that when His friends visited that tomb the body was gone ; that an angel declared that the body had been resurrected (Matt. xxviii: 6) ; that He appeared to His apostles with the body which had been crucified, even bearing the prints of the cruel nails in His hands, and the marks of the spear in His side, and to satisfy Thomas, He asked to be handled that no mistake might be made regarding its being a literal resurrection of the same body He had before the crucifixion (John xx: 27, 28). ، This was the resurrection of our Master, and inasmuch as He has commanded us to follow Him, why should ours not be the same?"

" But you will admit that if Christianity is true and Christ is really the Savior, that there is a great difference between His resurrection and that of those who have died since. His body had only just been interred; there had not been sufficient time for it to decay in the grave, and He was God Himself, while the bodies of others decay, and are scattered, in some cases at least, to the four winds," answered Brown.

" How about the statement regarding the

resurrection of others, who, the scriptures declare, came forth from their graves at the time of Christ's resurrection ? (Matt. xxvii: 52.) They certainly must have slumbered for a long time."

"I cannot understand," said Brown "how it could be possible for a literal resurrection of the body to occur after decay had taken place, and the body had returned as dust to the earth."

" Mr. Brown," the Elder said, "you will candidly admit that there are many things now accepted as truths which at one time seemed to you incomprehensible?"

" No doubt, I do," answered Brown.

"Yes, you do, most decidedly : For instance, when you first learned of the wonders of the telephone, you could scarcely credit them; when you were informed that you could converse with a friend who stood miles away, you not only doubted, but perhaps disbelieved, yet you doubt no longer, for your eyes have seen, and your ears have heard. . Is not this true?"

"It is ; what the eye has seen or the ear has heard, one must certainly believe. But is not that a vastly different proposition?"

"Not at all ; you are only less familiar with the methods or principles upon which the resurrection depends, that is all. When we have more of the intelligence of heaven, and can understand more regarding the great principle by which the resurrection is brought about, it will appear simple enough. God permits a ray of intelligence to come from heaven ; it reaches the mind of man, it gives us knowledge of the telegraph, by which our messages flash from nation to nation in the twinkling of an eye, and opens to our understanding many other wonders of modern science. We may not understand fully how it is done, but we know it is accomplished, and we therefore believe what we once disbelieved.

"Another ray reaches us, and we have an understanding of the telephone, the phonograph, the electric cars; and through the effects of these discoveries, we open our eyes in wonderment! Yet these flashes of intelligence are nothing compared with the mighty fire of wisdom in the heavens from whence these originate. They may be new to us, but are thoroughly understood by Him who sent them. They are all gifts from the Father of our spirits, and only small gifts at that, compared with what He has in store for us."

"How can you imagine for an instant," exclaimed Mr. Sutherland, "that it can be possible for all the particles of our bodies to be gathered together again after they have been scattered?"

"I do not, and cannot pretend to, answer this question. It will require more intelligence than I have, to answer it. But this I firmly believe ; that no particle, that is, none of the component parts, of my body will ever go to make up the body of anything else, except perhaps for a time, and that it matters not whether my body be burned or permitted to decay and return to mother earth, every particle will be collected and brought together again, at the time of the resurrection which will be literal in every sense of the word. Let me relate a little anecdote which illustrates my position.

" A person had received, as a birthday gift, a beautiful silver cup from a friend. This cup was prized very much, not only on account of its beauty, but because of the love the receiver had for the giver. In a short time the one making this present was called away, the cold hand of death was laid upon him.

"Then the cup increased a hundred fold in value to the owner, and nothing could influence him to part from it. Years afterward, the owner of the present carried it to the place where he was employed, for the purpose of exhibiting it to a fellow workman. During the day, in passing the shelf where it rested while he was engaged in moving some valuable goods, he carelessly knocked the cup from the shelf, and it fell into a vessel of fluid. Thinking at the moment that the vessel contained nothing but

13

water, the owner waited until his arms were
released from the valuable load they contained,
before seeking to remove the cup from the place
into which it had fallen. When he returned,
he found, to his sorrow, that his cup had disappeared. Upon investigation, imagine his sorrow, when he discovered that the vessel contained nitric acid instead of water, and that the
cup had been eaten up by the fluid. He thought
of how he had valued that keepsake, how much
he revered the memory of the giver, and how
foolish he was to bring the prize from his home
that morning. At this moment, his employer
happened along, and noticing his grief enquired
for the cause. After listening to the poor man's
story, and learning that the cup was made in a
neighboring town, he rather startled the sorrow-
ing man with this remark: 'Don't feel bad,
my man, I promise you shall again have your
cup.'

"The workingman, thinking his words meant
that he should receive the amount of its real

value, or another cup, explained that it was not
its cost, neither would another cup fill its place.
It was the loss of this particular article, which
came from the hands of a friend who had since
died, that caused him grief.

"'Never mind, I say, whether you believe my
words or not, I promise, and will make good that
promise, that you shall again have your cup,
and it shall be made of the same identical silver,
having the same form, and being composed of
nothing but the same metal. I don't mean the
same kind, but the very same silver you dropped
into that fluid.'

"And with this he took a few handsfull of
common salt, flung them into the liquid, and
there formed in the solution a white solid ; this
he removed, dried and heated in a crucible, and
the result was a lump of silver of the highest
lustre.

"'Now, you see,' said the kind-hearted man,
'how easy it is to restore when you understand
the method by which it is done. All the silver

composing that cup of yours is now in my hands. How easy it is for me to have it re-moulded in the same moulds! and who will say you have not the same cup resurrected from the grave ?'

" Can you not understand," said Durant, "that this laborer was in the same condition as the poor mortals who are in painful ignor-ance of the way and means by which the resurrection will take place ? And yet how simple when once understood. The cup had been buried in that world of liquid, it had dis-solved and had been scattered throughout the world in which it was buried, and to a person unacquainted with the laws governing such things, was lost forever. If man, who is as a babe compared with God in intelligence, could resurrect a cup from that little world, do you not think it possible for God, who is the foun-tain-head of intelligence and power, to restore your body after it has been scattered through-out this little world of ours ? And as the re-

storing of that cup appeared very simple to that
laboring man, so I believe the resurrection of
the body will appear very simple to us when we
are on the other side, and fully understand the
laws, methods and powers which govern the restoration."

At this moment a Mr. Williams, who had been
a very attentive listener during the entire evening, arose and said : "Mr. Durant, to all appear-
ances you have proved every argument made
with some quotation from the Bible ; your
mode of reasoning appears very logical, but I
have here a passage which seems to conflict
with the argument that baptism is positively
essential to salvation."

"If so," answered the Elder, "I will be
pleased to listen. Really, if you have found an
argument, from the sayings of Christ or His
apostles, which promises salvation without baptism, you have certainly made a great discovery."

" Well, I think the discovery has been made,''

answered Williams, "and it seems strange that a gentleman who has made the Bible as much of a study as you have, has never been able to comprehend it."

"Thanks, but now for the argument ; do not build your hopes too high, perhaps you misunderstand your own reading of the Sacred Record."

"Well, that remains to be seen. You have disclaimed all belief in death-bed repentance bringing salvation, and you are, as well, a disbeliever in salvation without baptism. Now to the law and the testimony once more. Examine the account of the crucifixion, as recorded in Luke 23rd chapter, beginning with the 39th verse. Christ upon that occasion had a malefactor on either side of Him ; one railed on Him saying, ' If thou be Christ, save thyself and us,' while the other, being filled with repentance and being converted, rebuked his companion in sin and implored the blessed Redeemer : ' Lord remember me when thou comest

to thy kingdom.' Christ, witnessing the repentance of this malefactor, even at the last moment
of his life, presented him with the gift of salvation before giving up the ghost : 'Verily I
say unto thee, today shalt thou be with me in
paradise.' These were the words used by the
Captain of our salvation ; the promise was
granted without baptism, and he was carried to
heaven with our Savior ; and yet in the very
face of this testimony you proclaim the doctrine
that without baptism salvation cannot be obtained."

"Christ did not offer that malefactor salvation on that occasion, neither was he carried to
heaven with the Redeemer. I desire to convince you, Mr. Williams, if you will accept
the statement in the Bible, and I believe you
will, that Christ did not go to His Father until
some time after this, and that the paradise referred to is not the haven of salvation that we
all hope to reach."

"Mr. Durant, if you convince me of this, I

will have nothing more to say," replied Mr. Williams.

"Very well, then, pay strict attention to the words you have just quoted which contain the promise that in your opinion insures the penitent malefactor entrance to the presence of the Father: 'Today shalt thou be with me in paradise.' Three days after these words were spoken, we discover Mary weeping as she bowed down at the sepulcher where Christ's remains had been deposited, and upon recognizing her Lord, who stood by her side and addressed her, she received this command, 'Touch me not, for I am not yet ascended to my Father.' Rather a strange and startling declaration for the Savior to make, was it not, when the promise to the thief, made three days previously was to the effect that upon that day they should both be in His presence?"

"Why, Mr. Durant," exclaimed Claire, "I can't understand it at all; He did certainly make the promise, and yet from His words, spoken three days after, it appears that He had not yet been to His Father. Can it be that one of our Savior's promises has really fallen to the ground unfulfilled?"

"Not in the least, Mrs. Sutherland; it is merely another one of those cases where we read but fail to understand. 'The letter killeth but the Spirit giveth life,' you know. Christ kept His word with the malefactor, and He also spoke truthfully to Mary. He and the sinner undoubtedly went on the day mentioned to paradise, but the great mistake, made by many, lies in believing that paradise is heaven."

"Well, if paradise is not heaven, what is it? If they went to some other place, where is that place?" exclaimed Mr. Williams. "I believe it was heaven."

" I do not doubt your statement for a moment. Prof. A. Hindercoper, a German writer, says: ' Ih the second and third centuries every branch and division of the Christian church, so far as their records enable us to judge, believed that

Christ preached to the departed spirits.' This
is in harmony with the belief of the Latter-day
Saints, as well as in harmony with the Bible.
Peter speaking upon this subject answers your
question by saying: 'For Christ also hath once
suffered for sins, the just for the unjust, that
He might bring us to God, being put to death
in the flesh, but quickened by the spirit: by
which also He went and preached unto the
spirits in prison; which sometimes were diso-
bedient, when once the longsuffering of God
waited in the days of Noah, while the ark was
a preparing, wherein few, that is, eight souls
were saved by water.' Christ undoubtedly
understood that His mission would not end with
His crucifixion, but as He finished His mission
to mortals by opening to them the gospel gates,
it would be the beginning of His mission, for
a similar purpose, with those on the other side
of the vail, and realizing that His mission there
would begin immediately upon His release here,
and that the malefactor would meet him there,

He made the promise mentioned : 'Today shalt thou be with me in paradise.' Peter declares that they were visited and preached to in order that they might be judged according to man in the flesh, but live according to God in the spirit. (I. Peter iv : 6.) Bishop Alford, speaking of the declaration made by the chief apostle, said : ' I understand these words (I. Peter iii : 19) to say that our Lord in his disembodied state, did go to the place of detention of departed spirits, and did there announce his work of redemption; preach salvation in fact, to the disembodied spirits of those who refused to obey the voice of God when the judgment of the flood was hanging over them."

"That seems reasonable, and it has given me a new idea and something to consider," said Williams, " but how about the ordinances you claim are necessary for all ? How can those who did not hear the gospel before they died, receive the ordinances ?"

" Now we believe that those who embrace

the gospel in the spirit world will be saved; and believe with the scriptures that a vicarious work must be performed for them by the living. This doctrine was evidently understood by the saints in the days of the apostles. Paul informs us that the first gospel ordinance of all dispensations, baptism, was administered by proxy among the former day Saints. While teaching the Corinthian saints about the resurrection, (I Cor. xv : 29) he asks them: ' Else what shall they do which are baptized for the dead, if the dead rise not at all?' in other words, of what use is baptism for the dead, if there is no resurrection? showing that the doctrine of baptism for the dead was evidently neither new nor strange to the people to whom the apostle was writing. Christ died for the dead as well as the living : " For to this end Christ both died, and rose, and revived, that he might be the Lord both of the dead and the living." (Rom. xiv: 9.)

" But do you mean that living persons shall be baptized for the dead?"

"Certainly. Before the great day of the Lord shall come 'that shall burn as an oven, and when all the proud, yea and all that do wickedly shall be stubble ; and the day that cometh shall burn them up, saith the Lord of Hosts, that it shall leave them neither root nor branch,' (Mal. iv : 1,) an important event is to take place, as we learn from the same prophet, verses 5 and 6: 'Behold I will send you Elijah the prophet before the coming of the great and dreadful day of the Lord ; and he shall turn the heart of the fathers to the children, and the heart of the children to their fathers, lest I come and smite the earth with a curse.' The coming of Elijah, to inaugurate this great work must evidently be to some one who is prepared to receive him. His mission, 'to turn the heart of the fathers to the children, and the heart of the children to their fathers' is very comprehensive, and pertains to the whole family of Adam, there being no discrimination between the living and the dead, between those who have lived in the .

past and those who shall live in the future. There must be a welding link between the fathers and their children, and that welding link is baptism for the dead. We testify that Elijah has come; that he appeared to Joseph, the seer, and Oliver Cowdery, in the Kirtland Temple, on the 3rd of April, 1836, and said: 'Behold, the time has fully come, which was spoken of by the mouth of Malachi, testifying that he (Elijah) should be sent before the great and dreadful day of the Lord come to turn the hearts of the fathers to the children, and the children to the fathers, lest the whole earth be smitten with a curse. Therefore, the keys of this dispensation are committed into your hands, and by this ye may know that the great and dreadful day of the Lord is near, even at the doors.' Ordinances for the salvation of the dead require temples, or sacred places, especially constructed for their administration; for this reason, we build temples, and also, that we may perform other ordinances for the dead and the living."

"I have heard that the organization of your Church is unusually complete. How is it organized?" asked one of the visitors present.

"It is organized on the foundation of Apostles and Prophets. We have therefore various quorums of these in the Church organized by revelation for the efficient and harmonious performance of church duties. There is the First Presidency, chosen from those who hold the High Priesthood and Apostleship, consisting of a President and two counselors. The duty of the President is to preside over the whole Church, and he is sustained by the whole people as a seer, a revelator, a translator, and a prophet."

"What is meant by Priesthood? You must have two Priesthoods then, as you speak of the High Priesthood, indicating there must be a lower one?"

"The Church is governed by the Holy Priesthood, which is divided into two grand heads—

the Aaronic or lesser and the Melchisedek or higher.

"'The Melchisedek Priesthood, so called because Melchisedek was such a great High Priest, and also to avoid the too frequent use of Jehovah's name, as this Priesthood was formerly called after the order of His Son,—holds the right of presidency, to receive revelations from heaven and to enjoy the spiritual blessings; while the Aaronic Priesthood, so called because it was conferred upon Aaron and his seed forever, holds the keys of the ministering of angels, and to administer in the outward ordinances of the Church. The offices of the Melchisedek Priesthood include Apostles, Seventies, Patriarchs or Evangelists, and Elders, and the Aaronic Priesthood includes Bishops, Priests, Teachers and Deacons.

" Next to the quorum of the First Presidency is the Twelve Apostles, then the High Council, the Seventies, the High Priests, the Elders, and the quorums of the Lesser Priesthood.

"Each calling has its own duties to be performed, and the organization is such that one does not come in conflict with the other."

The company now parted for the evening, each hoping that an opportunity might be given to hear the Elder again.

14

CHAPTER XII.

A BAPTISM AND A CONVERSATION ON MARRIAGE.

IT will be remembered that on the evening of Mr. Durant's speech in the Town Hall at Westminster, an old lady came to him at the close of the meeting and whispered a " God bless you " to him. The truths uttered by him had made a deep impression upon her and were working to bear fruit. She had now made application to be baptized, convinced, as she was, of the truths of the gospel, and that this servant of God was authorized, by direct calling from Him through revelation, to perform the solemn ceremony. It was agreed, therefore, that the baptism should take place on an afternoon some time before the day of his departure to his home in the West.

He made it a point to obtain a conversation with the lady, and show to her the importance

of the step she was about to take. It is no
simple or indifferent affair. It is a contract
with God, fraught with wonderful results, to the
person who makes it, that will either lead to
rich blessings or to condemnation. When one
man makes a contract with another, the breaker
of such a contract must be willing to suffer the
ignominy attending his deceit. In baptism,
the subject makes a solemn vow with his Creator, and, rising from the waters in which he is
buried in the likeness of the death of Christ,
he should thenceforth walk in newness of life,
and should not serve sin. He is made free from
sin, and becomes a servant to God, he has his
fruit unto holiness and the end is everlasting
life. (Romans vi.)

The earnestness of the new convert's faith
and repentance was inquired into, and it was
pointed out to her that she should prepare herself to receive the testimony of the Spirit, which
is made known to different individuals in different ways—not always by unusual manifestations,

but frequently by the calm self-consciousness of peace that comes from a performance of righteous acts, in which the Spirit bears witness with our spirit that we are the children of God, heirs and joint heirs with Christ. We must not look for approval from friends, relatives or people of the world, in taking this step, but be prepared to suffer with Christ that we may be also glorified with Him, and exclaim with Paul : "I reckon that the sufferings of this present time are not worthy to be compared with the glory which shall be revealed in us." (Rom. viii : 18.) Like Christ, one must bear the cross upon the lone way, full of hope, confidence and zeal, knowing that the end is everlasting life.

Having said this much, and given many other incidental instructions, that would thoroughly impress the new convert with the sacredness and importance of the step about to be taken, Mr. Durant, members of the Marshall family, and a number of strangers, anxious to witness the ceremony, made their way, on a pleasant afternoon, to a beautiful wood where a stream wound its clear, slow waters in fantastic forms to empty into one of the large rivers. The autumn tints, the sun casting its warm influence to the earth through the gray atmosphere, the rustle of the wind in the falling leaves, and the beauty of nature all around, made the scene grand and romantic. Some who had gone along to make sport of the "Mormon baptism," were awed into strange silence by the beauty of the scene, and by the solemnity and scripture-like simplicity of the ceremony. After a word of prayer had been offered, in which Mr. Durant invoked the blessings of God upon the ordinance about to be performed, and asked that all disturbing spirits might be banished, he took the lady by the hand and waded with her out into the water, and, in the stillness which followed (those upon the shore unconsciously remaining uncovered), he was heard to say, as he held the old lady's hands in his left, and raised his right hand into the air : "Julia Howard, having been

commissioned of Jesus Christ, I baptize you in
the name of the Father, and of the Son, and of
the Holy Ghost.   Amen."

Then he immersed her in the water, and both
came forth again out of the water.

The company soon dispersed, and upon arrival at her home, the new convert was confirmed,
she preferring this to having that ordinance
performed upon the water's edge, which is frequently done. Mr. Durant placed his hands
upon her head, and by virtue of his calling and
authority, confirmed her a member of the
Church of Jesus Christ of Latter-day Saints, and,
in the manner of the apostles of old, bestowed
upon her the gift of the Holy Ghost which he
promised should be a light to her all her days.

The Elder was about to leave, having welcomed the new member and congratulated her
upon the step she had taken, when he was
somewhat surprised by a remark she made in
which she expressed a desire to gather with the
Saints.

The spirit of gathering had already rested upon her, and he explained to her the importance of this principle of the gospel. The Father desires that His children shall be gathered in unto one place where their hearts shall be prepared against the day when tribulation and desolation shall come upon the wicked. The Psalmist referred to this subject and exclaimed: "Gather my Saints together who have made a covenant with me by sacrifice." (Ps. 1: 5.) Isaiah, looking to the future, saw that in the last days the mountain of the Lord's house should be established in the tops of the mountains to which all nations should go. (Isaiah ii: 2.) Here the Lord was to give them one heart, and make an everlasting covenant with them. (Isaiah xxxii: 37–44.) And in that day the Lord should set His hand again the second time to recover the remnants of His people. (Isaiah xi: 11-16.) John, the revelator, saw this time, and heard a voice from heaven saying: "Come out of her [Babylon] my people, that ye be not partakers of her

sins and that ye receive not of her plagues."
(Rev. xviii : 4.) It was, therefore, in strict
accordance with the scriptures that she should
have the desire to gather, as well as that the
Saints should have an assembling place where
they might learn to walk in the paths of God
more strictly than in the world. There are ordinances, too, to be performed in the holy temples, for the living and the dead, that cannot be
done elsewhere. It is not well, however, that
this act of gathering should be considered
thoughtlessly and in haste, but rather with
deliberation and careful forethought.

In the conversation, Elder Durant had incidentally remarked, that marriage was not only
for time but also for all eternity. The newly
wedded couple, Mr. and Mrs. Sutherland, who
had remained to witness the confirmation, were
naturally interested in this, and the subject was
further inquired into by them.

"What is the belief of the Latter-day Saints
in relation to marriage?" said Mr. Sutherland.

"We believe," said Durant, "that marriage is ordained of God, and is binding for eternity, when properly performed by a servant of God having authority."

"Then it would appear that you believe in the family relation continuing throughout eternity?"

"Certainly, why not? Everything that is done by the Lord receives the impress of eternity. That being the case, marriage, being sanctioned and ordained of Him, is also eternal if performed by one having power as the ancient apostles had, to bind on earth and it should be bound in heaven. It then becomes a work of God, and, as the Preacher exclaims : 'I know that whatsoever God doeth it shall be forever ; nothing can be put to it, nor anything taken from it.' (Eccles. iii : 14.) Can you think of anything more comforting than that the loving ties formed in this world are to endure throughout the ages of eternity?"

"It is certainly more pleasant than to dwell

upon a union that shall last only 'till death do
you part;' but what proofs have you that your
view of the matter is correct?"

"In the first marriage that was ever performed, when the Creator joined together Adam
and Eve as the parents of the human race, we
have no record of its being done to last only
'till death do you part,' and we do not learn
that He set any limit to the continuance of their
marriage relations.   Why should we doubt that
the gift of Eve to Adam, was designed to be
eternal?   They were married before the Fall,
before death came into the world.   They were
eternal beings not subject to death ; death was
not considered when God gave her to be his
companion and helpmeet.   Why then should we
conclude that death should void the contract or
separate them any more than that it should
destroy the spirit?   If their spirits could be
restored with resurrected bodies, why should
not the eternal work of God in joining them
as one remain unbroken?   The whole second

chapter of Genesis breathes the spirit of everlasting union between Adam and Eve. In the
eighteenth verse we are told by the Lord that,
'it is not good that the man should be alone.'
Adam, the man, was created an eternal being,
and when God said that it was not good for him
to be alone, we must conclude it was not good
that he should be alone in immortality ; so the
Lord gave him Eve for no particular period of
his life, but evidently, as she was also an eternal
being, to be his wife forever—the union to last
as long as they should last—eternally."

"That seems reasonable, and it is a pleasant
hope you have," said Claire.

"With us it is more than a hope ; it is knowledge. There are other passages of scripture
which bear upon the inseparable connection between man and wife, in marriage as ordained of
God. Paul (Eph. v : 22) says: 'The husband is the head of the wife even as Christ is
the head of the Church.' Christ remains forever the head of the Church, and even so the

husband remains the head of the wife eternally."

"What do you mean by saying 'in marriage as ordained of God?' Is not all marriage ordained of Him?" said Mr. Sutherland.

"By marriage as ordained of God, I mean marriage performed in the way He has appointed, by a man whom He has authorized to act in His stead. What man does of himself, without authority from God, must be like him limited to this life. Now, like the authority to baptize, this authority to marry in the way God has ordained, must come by revelation from Him, for no man can take these honors to himself. To find this authority, we must look for it among a people who believe in revelation, and not among churches who declare that the heavens are sealed, and that no further revelation is necessary."

CHAPTER XIII.

ABOUT THE MORMONS.

THE day upon which the Mormon Elder was to leave his missionary field to return to his home in the mountains, was rapidly approaching. Mr. Brown, the lawyer, had become so interested in the missionary and his peculiar people that this gentleman determined to accompany him to Utah, to see for himself what he had heard so much concerning.

On the evening before their departure, all the old friends were gathered at the Marshall residence, or hotel, and quite naturally the conversation turned to the contemplated trip to Utah, and from that to the motives which led the Mormons to settle in that territory.

" What were the considerations that led to the settling of Utah by the Mormons?" asked one of the members of the little company.

"Persecution by their enemies was the primary cause," said the Elder. "After the death of the Prophet Joseph, they were driven from their homes in Nauvoo, and hence sought a new abiding place in the West."

"How did the death of Joseph, the Prophet, occur?" asked Mr. Brown.

"He was murdered in cold blood by masked men. You understand that all innovations on existing conditions have been opposed from time immemorial. The gospel has particularly been combatted in all ages, as its history amply illustrates. The people of their time did not tolerate Christ and His apostles, and ceased not persecuting them as long as they lived upon the earth. They were all at last put to death. The truths which the Latter-day prophet taught were the same as were expounded by the Savior and his followers, and opposition to these came as naturally as that a similar cause produces a similar effect. The prophet was finally martyred for the testimony which he bore. He had been brought continually before the courts which, however, could prove no guilt against him, for he was innocent of any other offense than that of preaching the gospel of Christ, and bearing his testimony that the God of heaven had again spoken to man. Some three days previous to his assassination, he went to the city of Carthage, in Illinois, Nauvoo being then the abiding place of the Saints, to deliver himself up to the pretended requirements of the law. The governor of the state had pledged his word, as the chief executive, that the prophet should be protected, but no effort was made to fulfill this pledge, and so Joseph and his brother Hyrum were shot in Carthage jail, on the 27th of June, 1844, by an armed mob, composed of about two hundred persons who had painted themselves black."

"Did this murder of their prophet have the effect of discouraging the Saints, or rather, did they feel disposed to abandon the cause for which they had so far battled?"

" It is very natural that they felt discouraged and that some wavered in their course, but the great majority were inclined to continue with unfaltering zeal in the work, because they knew for themselves that the true gospel had been restored, and that they were engaged in the work of God. And here let me remark that the strength of the Church consists in the personal knowledge and testimony of the members. The Spirit of God fills each member with unfaltering faith, and he builds his superstructure of religious belief on personal knowledge, imparted to him, by the power of the Spirit, through revelation. This testimony remains as long as the person lives uprightly and honorably before the Lord, doing nothing to grieve it away. Instead of scattering and abandoning the Church, leaving it to die, as was expected and desired by its enemies, and which would doubtless have been the case if it had not been divinely established, the people gathered strength and, through the assistance of God, and the leadership of Apostle Brigham Young, forsook their homes in their beloved Nauvoo, crossed the trackless plains, scaled the mountains, and in the midst of a desolate wilderness founded a commonwealth which has attracted the attention and the admiration of the whole world."

"How did Brigham Young come to be the leader of the people?" asked Mr. Sutherland.

"He was the president of the Twelve Apostles, the quorum next in authority to the First Presidency, upon whom naturally rested the keys of the kingdom, upon whom, in fact, was conferred the power or authority that the prophet had received from on high. Sidney Rigdon and others sought the honor of leading the Church, but the Lord, through the manifestations of His Spirit, chose Brigham Young for the place, as president of the Twelve Apostles, the people sustaining him by their vote, at a meeting held in the grove near the temple at Nauvoo, on the 8th of August, 1844. He was

15

afterwards, December, 1847, chosen president of
the whole Church. He felt the power of his
calling, and made preparations for the great
exodus of the people to the West, which had
been considered during the lifetime of the
prophet, but which was now made absolutely
necessary by the persecution of the enemies of
the Church.   In 1845, anti-Mormon delegates
from nine counties of Illinois met, at Carthage,
and demanded the removal of the Saints.   The
Council of Apostles agreed to their demands,
knowing full well that there was no alternative
between exodus or extermination by massacre.
In February, 1846, the exodus began by the
Saints crossing the Mississippi River, the remnant following on September 17th of the same
year, and the movement triumphantly continued, with interruptions, under severest difficulties and hardships, until the pioneers, on
July 24th, 1847, entered the valley of the Great
Salt Lake.   Something of the hardships which
they endured, and of the magnitude of their

undertaking, the historians have graphically pictured. Tullidge says :

"'The Mormons were setting out under their leader from the borders of civilization, with their wives and their children, in broad daylight, before the very eyes of ten thousand of their enemies, who would have preferred their utter destruction to their 'flight,' notwithstanding they had enforced it by treaties outrageous beyond description, inasmuch as the exiles were nearly all American born, many of them tracing their ancestors to the very founders of the nation. They had to make a journey of fifteen hundred miles over trackless prairies, sandy deserts and rocky mountains, through bands of war-like Indians, who had been driven, exasperated, towards the West ; and at last, to seek out and build up their Zion in valleys then unfruitful, in a solitary region where the foot of the white man had scarcely trodden. These, too, were to be followed by the aged, the halt, the sick and the blind, the poor, who were to be

helped by their little less destitute brethren,
and the delicate young mother with her new-
born babe at her breast, and still worse, for they
were not only threatened with the extermination of the poor remnant at Nauvoo, but news
had arrived that the parent government designed to pursue their pioneers with troops,
take from them their arms, and scatter them,
that they might perish by the way, and leave
their bones bleaching in the wilderness. * * *
In the centuries hence, when the passing events
of this age shall have taken their proper place,
the historian will point back to that exodus in
the New World of the West, as one quite
worthy to rank with the immortal exodus of the
children of Israel.'

"Bancroft says :

"'Of their long journey many painful incidents are recorded. Weakened by fever or
crippled by rheumatism, and with sluggish
circulation, many were severely frostbitten.
Women were compelled to drive the nearly

worn-out teams, while tending on their knees, perhaps, their sick children. The strength of the beasts was failing, as there were intervals when they could be kept from starving only by the browse or tender buds and branches of the cottonwood, felled for the purpose.

"'At one time no less than two thousand wagons could be counted, it was said, along the three hundred miles of road that separated Nauvoo from the Mormon encampments. Many families possessed no wagons, and in the long processions might be seen vehicles of all descriptions, from the lumbering cart, under whose awning lay stretched its fever-stricken driver, to the veriest makeshifts of poverty, the wheel-barrow or the two-wheeled trundle, in which was dragged along a bundle of clothing and a sack of meal—all of this world's goods that the owner possessed.

"'On arriving at the banks of the Missouri, the wagons were drawn up in double lines and in the form of squares. Between the lines, tents

were pitched at intervals, space being left between each row for a passage way, which was
shaded with awnings or a latticework of
branches, and served as a promenade for con-
valescents and a playground for children.'

"But it would be too long a story, to follow
the exiles in their vicissitudes through the
whole of their weary march across the uninhab-
ited wilderness that lay between them and their
future home, in the then wild valleys of the
mountains, and to speak of their struggles for
existence after they arrived there. They passed
through many severe afflictions in building up
the country and in settling the territory. The
crops were often destroyed by grass-hoppers,
crickets, untimely frosts, and drought, but in
each difficulty, the Lord overruled circumstances
for good and prospered the people, providing
the necessaries of life. Settlements were established at various points north and south of Salt
Lake City, and the thrift of the people, sea-
soned with the blessings of God, soon caused

cities and villages to spring up in all directions. President Young, himself, often went to seek locations for these sites, and was very frequently present when a city or town was founded."

"Truly, a wonderful people with a strange and fascinating history. I am more enthusiastic than ever in my determination to see them and their gathering place," said Mr. Brown.

The evening was far spent, and the company prepared to retire, after the usual leave-taking on such occasions. They all wished the missionary and Mr. Brown a pleasant journey. The parting was affecting, for the people had learned to love the Elder, and he, in turn, had a strong and living interest in them. Many missionaries can testify of the binding influence such friends have upon their affections, and people who have learned to love the Elders are frequently as loth to part with them as with members of their own families. This case was no exception. Durant thanked them all for their kindness to him, and blessed them for their hospitality, expressing a desire to see them gathered with the Saints, if God should open their hearts to an adoption of the gospel truths.

Early on the following morning, the Elder and Mr. Brown set their faces to the West, and with the present facilities for travel, expected soon to be in the land of the Mormons. As they passed over the vast plains, large rivers, rolling and rugged hills, and pleasant valleys, their conversation was often directed to the great difference between travel as the pioneers endured it, and as it is now enjoyed in the trains of palace coaches.

On a pleasant Saturday evening, after a four days' journey, they arrived in Salt Lake City, where Durant met his family all feeling well. The meeting between husband and wife and children, after such a long separation, was happy in the extreme, and it was with thankful hearts that they kneeled by the family altar, praising God in fervent prayer for His kind mercies in preserving them to meet once more.

During the afternoon of the next day, Sunday, they all attended meeting, where an Elder delivered the following discourse, which Mr. Brown listened to with marked attention:

"MY BRETHREN, SISTERS AND FRIENDS :

"I am thankful for the privilege of speaking to you a short time this afternoon. I am anxious to explain, whenever opportunity affords, the nature of our faith.

"In this free country, where we congratulate ourselves in enjoying and allowing the greatest freedom to everybody, I presume we will, all of us, speaker and congregation, exercise the privilege of explaining and reflecting upon the things that may be said, so that our friends, I trust, will leave us understanding a little more about the nature of our religion than when they came to the meeting.

"Our visiting friends have, doubtless, heard

about the Latter-day Saints. They have had the opinions of men who have spoken in the pulpits, and who have written books about the Mormons, and they, very likely, have come here under certain impressions in regard to the Mormons' faith.

"I am sorry to say that experience has taught me that the public generally have been deceived. I am gratified sometimes in listening to acknowledgements of this kind from those who have heard for themselves, and have thus been able to judge intelligently as to whether the reports which they have heard from our enemies are correct or not.

"It seems strange, but it is nevertheless true, that many people who wish to know the faith of the Saints go to their enemies to learn of them. I do not know whether our kind friends have thought of the inconsistency and injustice of such a course as this. If I wished to learn what the Roman Catholics believed in, I do not think at present that I would go to the Protestant Church to learn it ; or if I wished to learn what any denomination of professing Christians believe, I do not think it would be just for me to go to some other denomination to ascertain it. In the first place, other churches might be led—perhaps unwittingly, perhaps intention- ally—to misrepresent the faith of their neigh- bors, and I might be deceived through their misrepresentations. On the other hand, there is no need of my going to any one church to learn the faith of another people, because I can go just as easily to their own church to listen to their explanations, and thus be sure of getting information of their peculiar views, without trusting to the misrepresentations of their neighbors. Now I submit that such a course as this is right ; it is just, and accords with our impressions of a fair and just hearing and con- sideration from the parties most interested, as to whether their faith be correct or not.

"Of course we have no disposition, as Latter- day Saints, even if we had the power, to con-

strain any person to believe our doctrines. We
have not the power ; we have not the disposition. We simply wish to explain the nature of
that religion of which we are ministers—laboring under a feeling of anxiety to deliver the
message with which we have been sent, that our
friends may have the privilege of receiving or
rejecting it, just as they think proper.

"I approach the examination of this subject,
because I believe that many of our kind, honest,
well-wishing friends—those who desire to serve
God according to His will and pleasure—are
under the impression that there exists a confusion so general, and errors so prevalent, that
religion seems to be losing its hold upon the
minds of the people. And, of course, we who
have faith in God and in His revealed word, as
contained in the Old and New Testaments, de-
plore a state of things that indicates a departure
from that respect and reverence which we wish
to see existing and manifested on the part of the
people towards the Supreme Being.

"What is the reason that people are becoming irreligious? What is the reason that people talk of sacred things lightly? What is the reason that men who have heretofore been respected as ministers of religion are now little thought of? It is simply because the religions that are taught are losing their hold upon the minds and affections of the people; because the religions that are taught do not supply the want that men and women feel; because the word preached by most ministers carries with it no power to convince people as to the truthfulness of the doctrines that are presented, or the sinful condition of the people to whom they are taught.

"The present condition of the Christian world does not present that union, that love, that we expect from the perpetuation of the doctrines that Christ taught, and it is this fact, understood by many, that increases their doubts and strengthens their objections to what is called 'Christianity.' The New Testament teachings lead us to expect a state of unity in the Christian Church. The admonitions of the Apostles were to the effect that the Saints in early days should be united together, that they should understand alike, that they should speak the same things, that they should be of the same mind and of the same judgment. Such are the words of the Apostle, to be found in I. Cor. i : 10.

"Now, my friends, does such a state of things exist around us in connection with the Christian churches that we might expect from the nature of a perfect religion, introduced by Christ? Does there exist, at the present time, a state of things so perfect as to agree with the expectations raised from the teachings of St. Paul in this scripture that I have quoted? I think not. I am safe, I believe, in stating—and I think our friends are prepared to agree with me—that there does not exist amongst the Christian denominations that unity and that oneness of faith, peace, kindness and love which, by reading the New Testament, we might expect to appear amongst them as the true fruits of Christianity. And it is upon this I wish to make a few remarks before proceeding to explain to you, from the Bible, the nature of our faith.

" Of course the existence of a number of denominations called 'Christian' cannot be denied. But we are told that all the Christian churches exhibit to us one church ; that if one denomination does not teach the whole perfect plan of religion revealed by the Lord Jesus Christ, all the churches put together do ; although there may be divisions existing amongst the members of these denominations. Unless we accept this view we must object to Christianity on the ground that we cannot find which of all the Christian denominations teach the truth. Here is one church called Christian that teaches certain doctrines, another more or less in its teachings contradicts them, a third teaches doctrines that are in conflict with the other two, and so we might go through them all, and speak in like terms of those who think honestly enough that they are serving God.

"Now, my friends, I will ask this question— First, Is it reasonable to suppose that God would sustain two distinct religious churches as His churches? Is it reasonable to suppose that God would set up two distinct religious bodies, the ministers of which teach different doctrines? After learning from the Bible so much indicating the anxiety of God's inspired servants for a time of perfect unity, I say it is not reasonable to suppose it. And just so long as two distinct religious systems exist, teaching different doctrines and preaching different principles, there exists a conflicting influence, divisions, feelings, perhaps very strong, if the difference in doctrine is very decided. If it is not reasonable, what are we to do? How can we account for such a condition of things?

"This leads to the position we occupy. We want to know something more.

"Is it true that the bodies called 'Christian' at present represent the Church of Christ? Or is it true that they have ignored some things belonging to the perfect doctrine of Christ, and taken as their guide, their own conclusions in regard to what is right, which leads to this division of doctrine? How is it? But I will endeavor to show that it is unscriptural, as well as unreasonable, for us to receive different Christian bodies as the Church of Christ.

"I will direct your attention to a few passages from the word of God. Jesus, when He sent the Apostles to preach in the first place, said to them, 'Go ye into all the world and preach the gospel to every creature.' Not *any* system that might be termed a gospel. There was no choice left to anybody. He spoke definitely in regard to the gospel plan, which He, the Son of God, came to the earth to set up. Paul, in the first chapter of Galatians, eighth verse, says, 'Though we or an angel from heaven preach any other gospel unto you than that which we have
16

preached unto you, let him be accursed.' Paul,
one of the Apostles, taught the gospel, the same
gospel that Peter, James, John and others
taught. They all taught the same system. And
Paul said, in another place, that he went up, by
revelation, to Jerusalem, taking Barnabas and
Titus with him, and communicated the gospel
which he preached among the Gentiles (Gal. ii:
1, 2), thus showing that he taught the same
thing everywhere. You see, Paul's words and
practice show that he did not admit of the
least change or alteration from the gospel as
taught by Christ, and preached by the Apostles
to the people. In another place it is said,
'Whosoever transgresseth and abideth not in
the doctrine of Christ, hath not God. He that
abideth in the doctrines of Christ, he hath both
the Father and the Son' (II. John ix.), showing
us that he taught strictly the necessity of abiding in that form of doctrine which had at first
been delivered. I quote these passages to show
you that the gospel which Christ and the Apos-

tles first taught was intended to be taught continually, without change, and that none had a
right, not even an angel from heaven, to preach
any other gospel than that which had been delivered at the first.

"Do you agree with this? Because I am
about to examine, in detail some of the doctrines that will readily show to you the difference between the ministers of the true gospel
and the ministers of the so-called gospel that
is preached at the present time. But are you
prepared to come to the conclusion, with me,
that it is the old gospel, Christ's gospel, the
doctrines of the apostles that we ought to seek
and follow, if we expect eternal life? Or do
you think you are safe in following the teachings of men, who have made great changes
from such ancient gospel, with the following
passage before you? "If there come any unto
you and bring not this doctrine, receive him not
into your house, neither bid him God speed."
(II. John 10th verse.) Do you think you can ob-

tain God's blessing by being members of a church or churches that teach doctrines opposed to what Christ taught ?   How is this ?

" ' Well certainly,' says one—a Bible believer —'of course I wish to have the religion of the Bible.   I would like to have the religion of Christ.   I do not admit of any departure.' This is right.   This is consistent.   Of course if there is a question as to whether God has made any change in His primitive faith, revealed through Christ, we shall consider it ; for I am willing also to make a change if God has authorized it.   I am quite willing to accept any doctrine that God has revealed from heaven for my salvation.   I confess to you that I have no disposition whatever to maintain private views or speculations which may have been engendered on my own part through reflection.   I wish the doctrine of Christ, as Christ taught it, as the apostles taught it, and I will not, with the light that I possess, depart one particle from the letter and spirit of that ancient plan.

And if there are any friends here who have
heard that the Elders of the Church of Jesus
Christ of Latter-day Saints do not believe in
the Bible, let them judge. There are no practices pleasing to God, or likely to bring His
blessings upon the heads of the children of men,
except those inculcated by Him, through His servants by the power of revelation from heaven, so
that we will not depart from the book. We will
not teach doctrines that are opposed to this book,
but we are prepared to show our friends, in the
spirit of kindness, that doctrines opposed to those
contained in this book are displeasing to God,
and are not calculated to bring peace and salvation to the children of men.

"'But,' says one, ' what matters it whether we
go this road that you point out or some other?
You know if we can get to heaven one way, is
not that as good as another? We will try to
illustrate this idea. If a man wish to go to
London, says the inquirer, may he not go the
road that leads towards the south, or a road that

leads towards the north, as the case may be;
what matters it so that he gets to London? It
would not matter in the least. He might go
the road that led to the north or that which led
to the south, and by making a shorter or longer
journey, as the case might be, he might get to
London. But you see there is no parallel between this figure and the facts in regard to
religion because there are not two ways to get to
heaven. That is the difference. There are two
ways to get to London probably, perhaps more,
but you see there is only one way to get to
heaven, so that when we admit, as an illustra-
tion, a figure of this kind, we start with an
error and it leads us astray.

"The Bible speaks of one way. It speaks of
two ways. It speaks of a broad road that leads
to destruction, and it speaks of a narrow way
that leads to eternal life. So you see there is
only one way that leads to heaven, and if any
one persuades us that the wide road will lead us
there, he deceives us, for there is only one way,

and it is narrow. The Bible is very plain upon this, because the doctrines are steadfast and sure, and the words are plain that there is but one way that leads to life and glory. Now that is the way we want to find out.

Jesus came, He said, to do His Father's will, not His own. He called Apostles and ordained them, and He said, "As I have been sent, so send I you. Go and preach the gospel to every creature." That was their business. But He said, 'Tarry ye first in Jerusalem, until ye are endowed with power from on high.' Jesus called the Apostles. He ordained them Himself. He instructed them personally, and He commissioned them to preach the gospel to every creature. But He wished them to tarry at Jerusalem until they received power from on high ; a certain gift which God had promised that they might be qualified, in every sense, to discharge the important duty devolving upon them, of administering words of salvation to a fallen world. The Apostles did this. They gathered in Jerusalem. They were there on the day of Pentecost, and whilst there, in the upper room, the endowment of which Jesus spoke was given unto them. The Holy Ghost came upon them, in the upper room, as a mighty rushing wind, and 'it sat upon them as cloven tongues of fire. And, whilst under that influence, the Apostles who were sent to preach the gospel, stood up, at least Peter did, as the mouth-piece of the rest, at that time to preach the gospel that Christ sent them to declare. Now, what was it? Let us lay a good foundation as we proceed.

"Were they qualified to preach it? I do not think any Christian will doubt it. If they were not prepared to teach the gospel of the Son of God, then I would have no hope, my friends, of hearing it in this life. Never. Jesus Himself chose them. He ordained them ; He instructed them, and after all this, as you will find in the 2nd chapter of the Acts of the Apostles, 1st, 2nd and 3rd verses, they assembled in

Jerusalem, and had fulfilled unto them the promise of the Lord Jesus Christ, receiving the endowment of which I have been speaking.

"I think that all my friends here are certainly prepared to accept the words that Peter spoke, and acknowledge them to be true. What did Peter say? First, he preached Christ and Him crucified. You see the people, who had gathered together on the day of Pentecost, were people, who had no faith in Christ. They had rejected Him and His instructions. They had been of those who persecuted Christ and the Apostles. They were of those who had either personally or in their sympathies sustained the crucifixion of the Lord Jesus. Therefore, Peter, knowing this, stood up and preached to them, first Christ and Him crucified, and he was successful. Who can doubt it? Peter, a servant of God, ordained by the Son of God. Peter, upon whom the Spirit of God rested as tongues of fire, as the scriptures have it. This man stood up and argued the point, and explained about Jesus. And who can doubt the result? I am sure we would have been disappointed if we had been told in the Bible that Peter was not successful. He was successful. Many believed on him, and the result of their belief was that they said, 'Men and brethren, what shall we do?" (Acts ii : 37.) No wonder they asked that question. People who had either helped to crucify the Lord, or who had rejoiced when He was crucified, as many of them did, to be convinced that that same Jesus whom they had assisted to crucify was indeed the Lord, the Christ ; and when they were convinced of this they cried out, 'Men and brethren, what shall we do?'

"Peter was prepared to tell them. He had the very instructions that were needed, and the words of Peter are applicable today, my friends, to you and to me, so far as we have not obeyed them.

"We are believers in Christ, I trust. We have fortunately made our appearance in this

life, in the midst of a people who at least believe in the divinity of Christ, and we have received impressions favorable to this end ; therefore the words of Peter, spoken to those who
believed in the divinity of Christ, are applicable to us, and are the words of salvation to us,
if that ancient gospel is not changed. What
were the words? He says, 'Repent and be
baptized every one of you in the name of Jesus
Christ, for the remission of sins, and ye shall
receive the gift of the Holy Ghost.' (Acts
ii : 38.)

"Was that the gospel? Yes, unless the Apostles disobeyed the instruction of Christ, because
they were sent to preach the gospel, and they
were endowed that they might preach it perfectly. and represent God, the Maker of heaven
and earth, in the words and spirit by which
they presented it unto the people.

"Now, my friends, faith in Christ was the
first principle of the gospel ; repentance of sins
was the second principle ; baptism for the re-

mission of sins was the third principle, and then
the reception of the Holy Ghost, by the laying
on of hands, as taught by Peter on that day in
Jerusalem.   Is there any objection to this?
' None at all,' says one, that is scriptural ; we
cannot object to it.'   A Bible believer cannot
object to it.   But what is becoming of us if
such doctrines are not taught?   ' Well,' says
one, are they not taught? '   No.   ' Faith in
Christ is taught,' and ' repentance of sins is
taught,' although by some people the latter is
taught first, before faith in Christ.   Some teach
that we must repent of our sins before we can
have faith in Christ.   This is a mistake.   We
cannot possibly repent of sin committed, unless
we are convinced that we have committed the
sin.   We cannot repent of laws broken, which
Christ has taught through His Apostles unless
we are first convinced that Jesus was divine, and
had the authority to teach them ; so that faith
in Christ and His divine mission must be the
foundation of our practice as Christians.   And

the first effect that faith in Christ produces, is
repentance of the sins which we have committed. So repentance is the second principle
of the gospel. But we differ a little more about
the third principle. Just read your Bible, and
you will find that Peter taught baptism for the
remission of sins (Acts ii : 38). Again, John
the Baptist, who was the forerunner of Christ,
baptized for the remission of sins (Mark i : 4).
'John was sent from God.' You will find this
in the 1st chapter of the gospel according to St.
John, 6th verse. John himself said, in the 33rd
verse of the same chapter, 'He that sent me to
baptize with water, the same said unto me,'
referring to the instruction he received from the
Father regarding Christ. Both passages assert
this, that John the Baptist was sent by God to
baptize with water, and we are taught in the
Bible that he did teach the baptism of repentance for the remission of sins. That is just
what we might expect. John was God's servant.
So was Peter. They both taught the same doc-

trine. John taught baptism, and Peter told the
people to be baptized every one of them. You
will remember the servant of God who was sent
to speak to Paul, to instruct him just after his
conversion. He went to him, and when the
scales fell from the eyes of Paul, or Saul, this
man of God said to him : ' Why tarriest thou?
arise, and be baptized, and wash away thy sins,
calling upon the name of the Lord " (Acts xxii:
16). Be baptized and wash away his sins? Yes.
Now, that agrees exactly with the doctrine of
Peter, and the doctrine of John the Baptist.
They were all three servants of God, and they
all taught the same doctrine, and those who
heard and believed that doctrine possessed the
selfsame faith ; so that so far as baptism is concerned, the ancient Saints did teach and practice
the selfsame doctrine—baptism for the remission
of sins.

"I want to talk a little about this. One says,
' Well, I have always been taught that baptism
was a doctrine of Christ anciently, but I have

been under the impression that it was not necessary to salvation.' That may be, my friends,
we have been taught a great many things, and
good Christian people have believed a great many
things that Christian people have rejected since.
But that is no reason why we should change
the Bible doctrine. The thing is right here.
' Well,' says one, 'I thought we were not able
of ourselves to do anything to help to save ourselves.' This requires proper understanding.
If baptism brings the remission of sins, and
baptism is not attended to by us, we cannot obtain the blessing. Certainly not. God gives us
bread to eat, but He does not present it to us.
A man sows seed in the ground and he sees to
it and he harvests it and it is threshed and
prepared and placed before us in the shape of
flour, but we have no disposition to deny that it
is the gift of God. If it were not for God's
goodness we should have no bread. If it were
not for the gift of God we could not attend to
the ordinance that brings remission of sins.

We have not power, of ourselves, to bring within our reach a single saving principle belonging to the plan of eternal life. It is all God's free gift. It is all in consequence of His mercy, and His charity, and His goodness and love, and pleasure manifested to us that we have any privilege at all that will help to make us better, or that will bring us into His Church and kingdom and give us a right to say that we are really His children. The fact that He has laid down ordinances, through which a remission of sins is brought to us does not warrant us in saying that we do it of ourselves, and when people talk like this it is likely to deceive.

"Now, my friends, the Bible says, in the place I have quoted, that baptism is for the remission of sins. Do we believe this? If we do, you know, we must also come to the conclusion necessarily that we cannot have a remission of sins without it. If God has placed the ordinance of baptism in His Church, as part of

His divine system for a certain purpose, the object cannot be obtained without it. The means which God reveals for certain purposes must be used. We cannot say, and it would be unreasonable in us to say, that when God speaks from heaven in regard to any particular thing, we can ignore His advice when we please and accept something that suits us. It is wrong, and it is this disposition that has led to the present deplorable state of things.

" 'Well,' says one, 'I have thought that baptism was for an outward sign of an inward grace, or of membership in the Church.' Another error, you see! The Bible does not say anything about that. Of course the act of a person embracing the principles of the gospel and becoming a member of the Church, may be a sign, but baptism was not set in the Church for that purpose. It was taught in the Church and administered for the remission of sins and nothing else. And no man or woman can obtain a place in God's kingdom, or enjoy His

17

presence here or hereafter, unless their sins are washed away in baptism, as Paul's were washed away when he accepted the advice of the good and inspired man, Ananias, who instructed him.

"When I think of the importance of this offer which God has made, my heart is filled with thankfulness instead of a disposition to discard what He has taught. It is strange, and we can only account for it on the ground of the waywardness of men naturally, to think that we would attempt to do things in opposition to the will of God. Is there a more important blessing offered to mankind than the remission of sins? Have we any hope of enjoying the glory of God in our present sinful condition? Surely not, for nothing sinful or unholy can enter the courts of glory. Then if God has so put in His Church an ordinance for the purpose of enabling us, like Saul, to wash away our sins, why not be prepared to receive it with joy instead of cultivating or encouraging a disposition to ignore it?

"Baptism for the remission of sins is the third principle of the gospel of Christ. Then comes the ordinance of the laying on of hands for the gift of the Holy Ghost. Peter says, on the day of Pentecost, to which we have directed your attention, ' And ye shall receive the gift of the Holy Ghost.' What did that consist of? The gift of God's Spirit. The reception of God's power, a portion of His power. The reception of an influence which leads those who possess it near to God in their feelings and in their faith. A feeling which produces not only that inward consciousness of acceptance with God as His son or daughter, but a power which gives outward manifestations of its divinity. Jesus did promise to the apostles when he sent them out first, that ' These signs shall follow them that believe.' Here are His words, ' Go ye into all the world and preach the gospel to every creature. He that believeth and is baptized shall be saved. He that believeth not shall be damned, *and these signs shall follow them that believe.'* The words of Christ, in the last chapter of Mark, 15th and following verses.

"'Well,' says one, 'you know we do not believe in miracles now. These signs were miracles, but we do not believe in them now.' That may be, my friends. This is the very reason why we are here, because there is such a great disbelief in the Bible; because there is a disposition to ignore the Bible; because there is a disposition to ignore the promises of Christ; and we wish to show you the things that are denied; we wish to point out to you the doctrines our fathers have denied; that our teachers have denied, and we wish to show you that they are in the Bible, the word of God, in the book which some have gone so far as to assert that we do not believe in. But is it true that the promises of God were fulfilled anciently in regard to this matter? Yes! In the 19th chapter and 7th verse of the Acts of the Apostles, you will find an instance related of the Apostles laying their hands on some that had been bap-

tized, and they spake with tongues. This was
one of the gifts that was manifested, in consequence of their receiving that spirit which produced them. See also Mark 16th and 20th.

You must not consider that, in teaching these
doctrines, we are advancing something of ourselves, something new. If we were teaching
new doctrine you would have a right to call us
to account and ask us for the proof. We are
teaching old doctrine. We are teaching the New
Testament doctrines, instead of those of our
Christian friends. We have no spirit of enmity
in the least degree, towards any living soul, and
when we refer to the faith of our Christian
friends remember, it is simply to make the difference between their views and ours more distinct to you. I say instead of our frinds calling
us to account, it is the Latter-day Saints who
have the right to come out and say to their
Christian friends, 'See here, why do you deny
signs which Christ said should follow believers?
What believers did Christ speak about? Why

believers in His gospel. He taught us that these signs should follow believers. Well then, if our Christian friends deny that, we have the right to call them to account. If Christ said that these miracles—manifestations of Almighty power—should follow the believers, I say what reason have you to deny it? The question is not now whether the Latter-day Saints possess the power or not. The question at issue at present is not whether the teachers of the Church of England have the power or not. The question is, Does Christ promise that power to believers in the gospel? I say He does, and I say that those who deny that such powers should follow believers, teach that which is contrary to the word of Christ and contrary to the facts that appeared in connection with the teachings and administration of the doctrines of Christ. So that it is not the Latter-day Saints that introduce a new doctrine, and we say to our friends, Hear us, we beseech you. Hear the message we have to deliver, for God has sent us to teach the old religion, the religion of Jesus, the simple plan which was revealed from heaven in ancient days, to save the children of men.

"Peter said, on the day of Pentecost, speaking of the gospel and its attendant blessings, 'for this promise is unto you.' That is, to the people who stood before him, ' to your children and unto all that are afar off even as many as the Lord our God shall call.'

" You see it was not confined to the members of the church in the first place, as some would have us believe. The promise of the laying on of hands for the gift of the Holy Ghost was made to the children of those who heard Peter, and to all who were afar off, even as many as the Lord our God should call. And if it be true that God is calling sinners to repentance now, we should see the same power manifested today, that is, if we have the true gospel. There can be no doubt of this.

" Which will you have, my friends, the doctrine of the Bible or the doctrines of men?

If you accept the doctrines of the Bible you
will have to become Latter-day Saints, and of
course that would be out of the question for a
good many. But we cannot find these doctrines
anywhere else, and that is a perplexity. What
shall we do about them? When I am speaking
to you I think of the position I occupied myself, when I heard the Latter-day Saints first.
I went to their meeting, not expecting to hear
anything that would interest me by any means,
but I heard the Bible doctrine taught. I could
not deny it. I found I had been mistaken. I
did not incline in my heart to fight against God,
but considerations came up. If I become a
Latter-day Saint, people will call me a Mormon.
If I embrace these doctrines, my friends will
point at me the finger of scorn. If I become a
Latter-day Saint my good neighbors will say I
am deceived and led astray, and that I have embraced a doctrine that is in opposition to the
teachings of Christ. Of course these things
flashed through my mind when I considered

and read the Bible to ascertain positively
whether these Mormons taught the truth or not.
I thought this—well ! I have been religious for
the purpose of making my peace with God, but
I have been mistaken and led astray by men
whom God had not sent to preach the gospel ;
but now I have found the truth, the old promises relating to God's power, all things as at the
beginning, have been restored, and I have the
promise of obtaining a place with the righteous,
according to the mind and will of my Heavenly
Father. Let friends say what they please, let
them say I am deceived, but I believe this Bible
is true. Let them say whatever they may in
regard to my faith ; no matter. I thought of the
time of Christ. They called Christ hard names;
and of the Apostles they spake a great deal of
evil. In fact the Bible says they called them
all manner of evil, and although I expected my
friends would denounce me, still when I thought
of what Christ had suffered, I was reconciled and
instead of fighting against God, I was willing

to accept His doctrine, in order to obtain His blessings.

"I state to you my friends that since the day I entered this Church I have rejoiced exceedingly. I have found proofs upon proofs. I have had reason to rejoice in consequence of the manifestations of God's power, confirmatory of the doctrines, and I can say that the Church of Christ is set up, its doctrines are taught, its practices are practiced, its promises are fulfilled, aud the evidences of its divine power are manifested in the midst of this people.

"I would like to say a few words in regard to another point. I have just said that I had been taught a religion by men whom God *had not sent*. I would like to explain. You will excuse us if we seem to be very extreme in our views. We have taken the liberty to teach you the truth, just as we have it, and when we say something that comes in coutact with what you have received, excuse us. There is uo bad feeling at all, or unfriendliness in the least. But we believe in persons being invested with the proper authority to preach the gospel. Paul says, speaking of the authority of the Holy Priesthood, 'No man taketh this honor unto himself, but he that is called of God as was Aaron.'" (Heb. v : 4.) 'Faith cometh by hearing, and how can we hear without a preacher?' (Rom. x : 14–17.) 'No man taketh this honor unto himself, except he be called of God as was Aaron.' Now that is very plain, and what does it mean? Simply what it says. That no man has a right to administer in the ordinances of religion except he be sent of God as was Aaron, for how can a man preach except he be sent? (Rom. x : 15.) If that be admitted, of course the next question of importance is, How was Aaron sent? By turning to the history we have of God's dealing with Moses, in reference to the gathering of the Israelites, from Egpyt, you will find that God instructed Moses to call Aaron to be his helper. (Ex. iv : 15, 16.) Here is the proof. No man can preach the gospel simply

because he feels inclined within himself to be
a preacher. No man can preach the gospel—
that is with God's approval and authority—
unless God commission him. God commissioned
every one of his preachers in ancient times.
He spoke from heaven. He directed those who
held this authority to call others. Christ called
the Apostles as He was called. His Father
called Him ; He called the Apostles, and He
said, ' As my Father hath sent me, even so send
I you." (St. John xx : 21). 'He that receiveth
you receiveth me; and he that receiveth me receiveth Him that sent me.' The authority was
here, you see. God called Moses; He instructed
Moses to call Aaron ; so that Aaron stood exactly in the same relation to God as did the
Apostles ; the latter being called of God the
Father through Christ. That would be evident,
because one whom God had authorized to act as
His servant was instructed by Him to call
Aaron. Now, you observe, no man has a
right to exercise the authority of the priest-

hood unless he is called of God as was Aaron.

"Are the preachers—those who commonly preach in connection with the churches of the present day—called of God as was Aaron? Or, in other words, are they called by revelation from God? This is the question. We do not doubt the propriety of their being called in this way, because the Bible says they ought to be. Do our Protestant ministers, at the present time, profess to be sent of God as was Aaron? Is there a minister connected with the Christian denominations of the present day who professes to be sent of God by direct revelation? Not one. It does not require any argument at all. They do not profess that they have heard from God. They say that God has not spoken since the last book of the New Testament was written. They say it is a sin, and they find fault with the Latter-day Saints because we believe that God does speak; that He has a right to speak; and it is necessary we should have His approval and commission in order to qualify us to attend to the business of His Church. So that our present Christian teachers do not profess to be called of God as was Aaron. They deny all revelation at present, or since the Bible was written.

"You know the ministers, among their other errors, receive pay for preaching. That is an innovation also. The ancient apostles, and seventies, and bishops, and so on, were not paid for preaching. But our present ministers are. The preachers of this Church, with whom I am connected, are not paid for preaching. They preach without money, without purse, and without scrip. Now the preachers of the present churches make a business of preaching. They learn to be preachers. They are brought up to be preachers in consequence of their parents or guides finding in this way a place where they may make a living. Such ministers sometimes acknowledge one kind of revelation. Not that God tells the people about His will, or that He manifests His power, but they sometimes tell us they have received a call from one congregation to another. But there is one peculiarity about it, viz: the congregation that calls them is a congregation that almost invariably offers them more money than the congregation to which they have been attached. This is the only instance of any kind of revelation being acknowledged by our Christian teachers. God has not spoken, say they, by inspired men, since the days of the ancient apostles. He has not spoken directly to the church. He has not authorized a single man to preach, but sometimes a call is given from less money to more. And though they are feeling full of love and affection for the congregation with which they have labored for years, yet they are sorry and regret so much that that call must be heeded, which takes them from among their old friends to a new congregation. But, you see, the new congregation offers the most money, and that cannot be disregarded.

"My friends, these are a few of the doctrines the Church of Jesus Christ of Latter-day Saints. Are we displeased with anybody? No, not at all. All are at liberty to believe what they please. But we are placed under obligations to deliver the message which God has sent. We say we are not solely dependent on the Bible, because God has sent the gospel. We do not wish you to think that we regard the Bible lightly. Of course you will have noticed, from our remarks, that this is not so. But we say from the Bible alone we could not have discovered the true way of life, any more than thousands of our friends have been able to do so. Why millions of people have read the Bible but have not discovered some of these doctrines. They have been lead to preach the things contained therein, and if they had discovered the doctrine, this Bible cannot lay on hands for the gift of the Holy Ghost. That part of the work that is necessary for man's salvation must be done by one whom God authorizes. Therefore the Bible alone is not sufficient. It contains the truth. It is the word of God. It contains the instruction of the apostles. But it does not contain the divine authority that is necessary to commission a man to baptize or administer in any ordinance pertaining to the house of God.

"Now, my friends, may God bless you. And my brethren and sisters, may the Holy Spirit, which leads unto all truth, abide upon us, and may we who have found the truth have a disposition to retain it. May we have the moral courage to say, 'Let God be served. Let His truth be obeyed.' Let the Almighty be honored, and if other people choose to follow their own fancies, or the deceptions presented before them by men whom God has not sent, as for us and our house, let us serve God.

"May God bless us, in the name of Jesus Christ. Amen."

CHAPTER XIV.

MR. BROWN'S LETTER TO THE MARSHALLS.

MR. BROWN soon became acquainted with a number of leading Mormon Elders who informed him more concerning the history of the peculiar people, among whom he was a visitor. The sights in and around the city were viewed by him, and he had time to inspect the most important buildings and places of interest. According to promise, he wrote a letter to the Marshalls giving some of his impressions of the country and the people, and his epistle is here reproduced in full :

DEAR FRIENDS :

"I am at length in the land of the Mormons— in the city of the Saints by the dead sea of America. I have been well received, and am pleased beyond measure with what I have seen and heard.

"It is a wonderful West. Our country as a whole surpasses the inexperienced conception of Europeans, and places their cramped-up districts, and tiny, although beautiful nations, in the position of play-things when compared with the vastness of America—rustic, rough, and rude as even its oldest places appear. Then what shall we say of the wide West—until recently an unknown region—with its variety of natural wonders, its wild mountains, appalling peaks and lonely valleys, industries, mines of wealth, gorges, streams, plains! It is grand, notwithstanding its development is yet in its infancy. Its possibilities for future greatness are inconceivable even to the hardy pioneer.

"We came over the Chicago Rock Island and Pacific Railway from Kansas City, *via* Denver. The State of Kansas, with its beautiful eastern cities, and its wonderful plains and new and thriving settlements in the western part, was presented to our view from the comfortable palace coaches of this well-equipped road.

"From Denver, where one sees the Rocky Mountains, cloven with fantastic ravines, and horrible chasms, dressed with rough and shaggy woods, and capped with everlasting ice and snow, we proceeded to Pueblo, and thence over the Denver & Rio Grande Railway, to Grand Junction, Colorado. It is no exaggeration to say that the mountain scenery along this route is the most magnificent in the world; while the mid-continent region, which this road traverses, is doubtless the most picturesque portion of our country. Very appropriately, this road, with its western connection—the Rio Grande Western—has been named, 'The Scenic Line.'

"Having passed Grand Junction, we soon enter Utah, and find ourselves in a country of bluffs, cliffs, wonderful formations, and deserts, which become wearisome in spite of the novelty of the scene. Nothing, however, could be more romantic than the worn battlements and rocky tablets, between which, for miles and miles, the road winds its way. Nearing Castle Valley, we attained a higher level, where the cliffs came nearer and were more precipitous, with the spaces between more green.

"We are climbing towards the heights of the Wasatch—the western bulwark of the Rockies just passed. Ahead is the Castle Gate, 'the most inspiring as a single object, of all the marvelous scenes between the plains and the Salt Sea.' We soon entered fairly into the Spanish Fork Canyon, the sides of which are neither rough nor cliff-bound, but, rather, are steep and rounded, covered with soft walls of greenery, and groves of aspen and oak. Nearing the valley, we beheld Mt. Nebo, over-topping other pyramids of the Wasatch range. Westward lies the volcanic mountain ranges and the arid deserts of Utah and Nevada; but at our feet, stretches forth a lovely valley, with the fresh, clear waters of the Utah Lake in the center.

"We passed on through miles of fertile

farmland, and between us and the pretty lake were fine meadows, upon which sleek herds were grazing. A semi-circle of Mormon settlements lie at the feet of the emcompassing hills, except upon the western side, where no water is found. Provo is the largest of the cities in this valley. A short ride, and we crossed the summit of a low mountain range, separating the valley, we had just passed over, from the the Great Basin. The train followed along the Jordan river which empties the waters of the Utah Lake into the Great Salt Lake. Salt Lake Valley lies before us, with the city of the Saints, and the wonderful saline sea to the north, the peaks of the Wasatch, to the north and the east; and about us, on every side, the marks of industry, thrift and prosperity, set in a framework of surprisingly beautiful scenery.

"The valley is extremely pretty when seen at the best season of the year. In autumn, when Nature, by the early frosts, has delicately tinted the leaves with brilliant hues, the mountains

and the hillsides are very attractive; the contrast between the vegetation of the hills and the
colors of the valley, is an interesting feature in
the panorama spread before the delighted ob-
server.

"Utah contains a population of about 200,000 ;
it has an area of 85,000 square miles, much of
which is mountains. The Great Salt Lake is
about forty by ninety miles in size, and contains
several islands. Fish abound in the numberless
small streams that flow from and through the
picturesque canyons of the Wasatch.

" The sterility of the country was removed by
a system of irrigation from the mountain
streams which fertilized the earth, causing it to
yield in abundance, and to 'blossom as the
rose.'

"When you remember the population and the
area, it will readily appear that there is great
room for more inhabitants, and yet it must be
remembered that only a small portion of the
ground is fit for cultivation, the greater part

being wild hills or sandy desert. The numerous valleys are like fruitful oases in a wilderness of rugged mountains, which latter serve as reservoirs for the snows of winter, that supply the summer rills with water.

"The valley, sometimes called the Great Basin, has an elevation of from four to five thousand feet, being surrounded and intersected by mountain ranges, which rise from five to seven thousand feet above the level of the basin. The Wasatch range extends along the east side of the valley ; at its western base is a narrow strip of land, the most fruitful in the Territory. In many other parts the soil is alkaline and sterile. In other districts there are fertile basins, with soil of good quality, yielding in places from fifty to ninety bushels of grain to the acre. There are immense deposits of coal, iron, and other valuable minerals, among them being gold, silver, copper, zinc, lead, sulphur, alum and borax. Salt works have been established in different places along the shores of the great lake, the water of which contains about 16 per cent. solid matter, 97 per cent. of which is common salt. In the chasms and ravines of the mountain streams are found cedar, pine, quaking asp, oak and maple, but timber is difficult of access. This, however, is compensated for by the immense deposits of coal in the neighborhood, and in the Territory itself, and by the railroad facilities the Territory now enjoys for shipping timber from Oregon and California.

"The hardships of early times, which are now well-known in history, have given way to prosperity, and the hidden resources of the hills and dales are appearing to bless the children of the Mormon pioneer. Thriving towns and cities extend from north to south, from east to west, over the whole territory, and Mormon colonies are planted along the Rocky Mountains, from Mexico in the south, to Canada in the north. Their industry is proverbial ; they view the building of cities, hamlets and villages as a divine call, taking hold of the often perilous labor with the invincible determination born of religious zeal and duty.

"Salt Lake City has a population of about fifty thousand, but it must not be understood that all these are Mormons. The tide of prosperity that has come to this people, has brought with it thousands of citizens from all parts of the United States, until the population is as mixed, in a religious sense, as that of any of the states of the Union; churches of all the Christian denominations, the halls of the agnostic, the synagogue of the Jew, and the gathering place of the infidel, are alike represented.

"Among the buildings of interest, in Salt Lake City, is the tabernacle, a remarkable edifice, and the great center of attraction. It was completed in 1870, is an oval-shaped building, with a major diameter of 233 feet, and a heighth of 70 feet, having a huge dome-shaped roof resting on pillars of sand stone. It seats about nine thousand people, and contains one of the largest organs in the world. Here services are held every Sabbath, when the Elders of the Church, leaders of the people, instruct the gathered thousands in the religion which, to my mind, is the only scriptural one now preached, and certainly the only one among them all having practical life and vitality It contains the germs of power that will leaven the whole religious world, scoff and deride as they may.

" The famous temple, erected at a cost of several millions, begun in 1853, now nearly completed, is built of gray granite, with walls more than six feet in thickness ; It has a length of 200 and a width of 100 feet ; the main walls rise to a height of 100 feet ; there are three towers and numerous minarets, on each end of the building, the center east tower being surmounted by a figure representing an angel blowing a trumpet, proclaiming the restoration of the gospel in the latter days. The cap-stone was placed on this tower, amid great rejoicing,

in April, 1892, when it was decided to finish the
building, and dedicate it in April, 1893, the occasion of the annual conference of the Church,
which is also the anniversary of its organization
(April 6th, 1830) in New York State, with six
members.   This great building is of elegant
design, grand proportions and unique pattern, a
marvel of beauty, strength and solidity.   Temples, of which there are several in the Territory—one in Logan, one in Manti, one in St.
George—are designed for use in performing
holy ordinances for the living, and vicarious
work by the living for the dead, as you understand the faith of the Saints, and as Elder
Durant has often referred to and explained in
his conversations with you.

" A Stake is a division of the Church, presided
over by a council of three High Priests, and in
Utah generally corresponds geographically to
the division of counties, while in other states and
territories, it often embraces larger districts.
The stakes are divided into wards, in each of

which a bishop and his two counselors exercise supervision. These again are subdivided into districts where presiding Elders or teachers look after the interests of the Church members. There are thirty-three stakes of Zion, with something over three hundred wards. Each stake has a general assembly building, while each ward, besides, has a structure for religious worship. The Assembly Hall, erected at a cost of $90,000, dedicated January 9th, 1882, erected near the temple, is the meeting place for the Salt Lake Stake of Zion. Much like a church in appearance, it is 120 by 68 feet in size, seating three thousand people, and is one of the most conspicuous buildings in the city. The walls are built of rough-hewn granite taken from the same quarrie that has supplied material for the temple.

"There are many other fine buildings in the city, besides natural attractions, as, for instance, Garfield Beach, where bathing is the pleasantest in America, the Hot Springs, the Warm Sul-

phur Springs, the gas wells, etc. There are
seventy miles of electric street railway, and a
hundred miles of streets. These avenues are
132 feet in width, having in many places rows
of shade trees on either side. Salt Lake City
covers as large an area as many other cities with
five times its population, and, excepting the business part, is largely composed of villas.

" Other principal cities are Ogden, Logan and
Provo. Ogden, thirty-seven miles north of Salt
Lake, is the railroad city of the territory, and
shows the results of the thrift and industry of
its inhabitants on every side. Many beautiful
natural attractions surround it—its warm springs
and rugged canyons being admired by all who
see them.

"But I have not space in this already long
letter to describe the mines, the manufacturing,
industrial and commercial establishments which
abound in this city and in the territory. Neither can I take time to more than merely refer
to the schools, public and private, and to the

educational facilities of the people. It has often been asserted that the Mormons are opposed to education, but the schools in every hamlet and city bear witness to the falsity of the assertion. No territory or state of the Union, of equal age with Utah, has finer school buildings, or is more advanced in matters of education, and to the Mormons may be ascribed the honor of having built and heartily supported the system that has made this possible.

"I see on every side among the Mormons, people who are honest in their convictions, who have a living faith and put their faith and teachings into practice, who are industrious and thrifty, kind to the poor, sober, virtuous. There are no signs of abject poverty anywhere in this city, and much less among the hundreds of country settlements ; idleness is discountenanced by the Mormons, until among them as a people there are no beggars, tramps or drones.

"A few more words, and I will not tire you with more this time. While, of course, I do not agree with all the doctrines of the Church, I consider the people as a whole are fair minded, and broad in their views. I have met the chief men of the Mormon Church, and have had a number of pleasant interviews with them. I find them men of grave and reverend demeanor, very religions in thought and deed, but not given to cant. They have not the sanctimonious airs that are so frequently noticed in religious ministers. Wilford Woodruff is the present head of the Church, the fourth man who has occupied that position—his predecessors having been : Joseph Smith, Brigham Young and John Taylor.

"Mr. Woodruff is several years beyond four score, but is hale and hearty, very affable in manner and interesting in conversation. He is a man of sturdy build, with a kindly, honest, intelligent face, and a manner especially winning and agreeable. You know that I have contended that the leaders of this movement were insincere, but when I met them and talked with them, when I marked the unwavering faith of that good, venerable old man, I changed my mind. In some things, he may be mistaken, but he is an honest worshiper of God.

"I must not close without remembering Mr. Durant to you. He was overjoyed to find his family all well upon his arrival. During my stay in this territory, I have remained at his home a part of the time, and have been very kindly treated.

"With love to all, I am your friend,

"WALTER T. BROWN."

CHAPTER XV.

CONCLUSION.

KIND reader, a word before we separate : if you are not a member of what is commonly called the Mormon Church, having read the foregoing pages, you must certainly acknowledge that you know more concerning its doctrines, from a Mormon standpoint, than you ever knew before.

We have tried to present to you, in a plain and very simple manner, some of the first principles of our faith, the true gospel of Jesus Christ. What do you think of them? Will they, or will they not, stand scrutiny? It is left with you to answer, and as God has blessed you with free agency, it is your privilege to judge and decide.

Do not treat these doctrines indifferently, nor carelessly throw them aside. Should they be true, the message is of the utmost importance to you. Surrounded with so many proofs, the faith of the Latter-day Saints should demand your further investigation.

Books, tracts, and sermons, in great numbers, and within easy reach, are at your command. Read, listen, investigate ! Thousands have done so before, and bear testimony to having received a knowledge of the divine truth, as herein presented.

I part from you with the words of the poet— true as any to be found :

"Know this, that every soul is free,
  To choose his life and what he'll be,
  For this eternal truth is given,
  That God will force no man to heaven.

" He'll call, persuade, direct aright—
  Bless him with wisdom, love, and light—
  In nameless ways be good and kind,
  But never force the human mind.

" Freedom and reason make us men;
  Take these away, what are we then?
  Mere animals, and just as well
  The beasts may think of heaven or hell."

APPENDIX.

WHAT BRIGHAM YOUNG SAID.

It is not only a privilege, but a duty for the Saints to seek unto the Lord their God for wisdom and understanding, to be in possession of the spirit that fills the heavens, until their eyes are anointed and opened to see the world as it really is, to know what it is made for, and why all things are as they are. It is one of the most happifying subjects that can be named, for a person, or people, to have the privilege of gaining wisdom enough while in their mortal tabernacle, to be able to look through the whys and wherefores of the existence of man, like looking through a piece of glass that is perfectly transparent; and understand the design of the Great Maker of this beautiful creation. Let the people do this, and their hearts will be weaned from the world.—Journal of Discourses Vol. I.,p. 111.

This people are to the world an object of derision and hatred; to God, of care and pity.—J. of D. Vol. V., p. 350.

There is not a person in this community that can bring to mind or mention the time when I exhibited one particle of sorrow or trouble to them. I calculate to carry my own sorrows just as long as I live upon this earth; and when I go to the grave, I expect them all to go there, and sleep with me in silence.—Journal of Discourse, Vol I., p. 31.

If people act from pure motives, though their outward movements may not always be so pleasant as our traditions would prefer, yet God will make those acts result in the best good to the people.—J. of D. Vol. V., p. 256.

No man can be exalted unless he be independent.—Journal of Discourses, Vol. I., p. 111.

There are but few of us but what have been honored with as convenient a place for a birth as was Jesus.—J. of D., . Vol. IV., p. 131.

You remember reading in the last book of the New Testament, that in the beginning God cursed the earth; but did He curse all things pertaining to it? No, He did not ;curse the water, but He blessed it. Pure water is cleansing—it serves to purify; and you are aware that the ancient Saints were very tenacious with regard to their purification by water. From the beginning the Lord instituted water for that purpose among others. I do not mean from the beginning of this earth alone; and although we have no immediate concern in inquiring into the organization of other earths that do not come within reach of our investigation, yet I will say that water has been the means of purification in every world that has been organized out of the immensity of matter.—J. of D. Vol. VII., p. 162.

The blood will not be resurrected with the body, being designed only to sustain the life of the present organization. When this is dissolved and we again obtain our bodies by the power of the resurrection, that which we now call the life of the body, and which is formed from the food we eat and the water we drink, will be supplanted by another element; for flesh and blood cannot inherit the kingdom of God.—J. of D. Vol. VII., p. 163.

If we accept salvation on the terms it is offered to us, we have got to be honest in every thought, in our reflections, in our meditations, in our private circles, in our deal, in our declarations, and in every act of our lives, fearless and regardless of every principle of error, of every principle of falsehood that may be presented.—J. of D. Vol. V., p. 124.

There is no such thing as a man being truly rich until he has power over death, hell, the grave, and him that hath the power of death, which is the devil.—J. of D. Vol. I., p. 271.

All men should study to learn the nature of mankind, and to discern that divinity inherent in them. A spirit and power of research is planted within, yet they remain undeveloped.—J. of D. Vol. VII., p. 1.

I am hated for teaching people the way of life and salvation—for teaching them principles that pertain to eternity, by which the Gods were and are, and by which they gain influence and power. Obtain that influence, and you will be hated, despised, and hunted like the roe upon the mountains.—J. of D. Vol. VII., p. 3.

Never accuse a man or a woman of evil, until you find out the cause. Never judge by the outward appearance.—J. of D. Vol. V., p. 169.

Do not get so angry that you cannot pray; do not allow yourselves to become so angry that you cannot feed an enemy.—J. of D. Vol. V., p. 228.

Do not offend God by not doing as He wants you to.—J. of D. Vol. V., p. 236.

If you could crowd an individual or a community into heaven without experience, it would be no enjoyment to them. They must know the opposite; they must know how to contrast, in order to prize and appreciate the comfort and happiness, the joy and the bliss they are actually in possession of.—J. of D. Vol. V., p. 294.

We have to learn to submit ourselves to the Lord with all our hearts, with all our affections, wishes, desires, passions, and let Him reign and rule over us and within us, the·God of every nation; then He will lead us to victory and glory; otherwise He will not.—J. of D, Vol. V., p. 352.

There is only one thing to fear, and that is, that you will not be faithful to the kingdom of God.—J. of D. Vol. V., p. 228.

My Christian brethren in the world say it is a piece of folly—a species of extreme nonsense, to believe that water will wash away sins. It is no matter to me what they say; it is a commandment of the Lord; there is no mistake in it, it tells for itself. He says, Do thus and so, and your sins shall be washed away. I care not how they are taken away; whether an angel takes them to the Lord to get forgiveness, whether they sink to the bottom of the stream, or float on the top, and be scattered to the four winds; He says, *Go into the water and be baptized, and they shall be washed away*; which is enough for me.—J. of D. Vol. I., p. 239.

When the wicked have power to blow out the sun, that it shines no more; when they have power to bring to a conclusion the operations of the elements, suspend the whole system of nature, and make a footstool of the throne of the Almighty, *they may then think to check Mormonism in its course*, and thwart the unalterable purposes of heaven. Men may persecute the people who believe its doctrine, report and publish lies to bring tribulation upon their heads, earth and hell may unite in one grand league against it, and exert their malicious powers to the utmost, but it will stand as firm and immovable in the midst of it all as the pillars of eternity.—J. of D. Vol. I., p. 88.

The time will come when the kingdom of God will reign free and independent. There will be a kingdom on the earth that will be controlled upon the same basis, in part, as that of the Government of the United States; and it will govern and protect in their rights the various classes of men, irrespective of their different modes of worship; for the law must go forth from Zion, and the word of the Lord from Jerusalem, and the Lord Jesus will govern every nation and kingdom upon the earth.—J. of D. Vol. V., p. 329.

Keep your spirits under the sole control of good spirits, and they will make your tabernacles honorable in the presence of God, angels, and men. If you will always keep your spirits in right subjection, you will be watching all the time, and never suffer yourselves to commit an act that you will be sorry for, and you can see that in all your life you are clear. Do not do anything that you will be sorry for.—J. of D. Vol. V., p. 328.

The Lord will not reveal all that we at times wish Him to. If a school master were to undertake to teach a little child algebra, you would call him foolish, would you not? Just so with our Father; He reveals to us as we are prepared to receive.—J. of D. Vol. V., p. 330.

The philosophers of the world will concede that the elements of which you and I are composed are eternal, yet they believe that there was a time when there was no God.—J. of D., Vol. I, p. 5.

You will find that this probation is the place to increase upon every little we receive, for the Lord gives line upon line to the children of men. When He reveals the plan of salvation, then is the time to fill up our days with good works.— J. of D., Vol. I, p. 5.

When you embark to fill up the end of your creation, never cease to seek to have the Spirit of the Lord rest upon you, that your minds may be peaceable, and as smooth as the summer breezes of heaven. Never cease a day of your life to have the Holy Ghost resting upon you.—J. of D., Vol, I, p. 69.

When I have served my God and my brethren, when I have performed every act required of me, *until nothing remains to be done, but to lie down and rest*, to seek recreation, then it becomes my lawful privilege, and not before.—Journal of Discourses, Vol. I., p. 112.

If you want to apostatize, apostatize, and behave yourselves.—J. of D., Vol. I, p. 84.

The duty of the mother is to watch over her children, and to give them their early education, for impressions received in infancy are lasting. You know, yourselves, by experience, that the impressions you have received in the dawn of your mortal existence, bear, to this day, with the greatest weight upon your mind. It is the experience of people generally that what they imbibe from their mothers in infancy is the most lasting upon the mind through life. This is natural, it is reasonable, it is right. I do not suppose you can find one person among five hundred who does not think his mother to be the best woman that ever lived. This is right, it is planted in the human heart. The child reposes implicit confidence in the mother, you behold in him a natural attachment, no matter what her appearance may be, that makes him think his mother is the best and handsomest mother in the world.—J. of D., Vol. I, p. 67.

I never passed John Wesley's church in London without stopping to look at it. Was he a good man? Yes; I suppose him to have been, by all accounts, as good as ever walked on this earth, according to his knowledge. Has he obtained a rest? Yes, and greater than ever entered his mind to expect; and so have thousands of others of the various religious denominations.—J. of D., Vol. VII., p. 5.

Persecution and hatred by those who love not the truth are a legacy bequeathed by the Savior to all his followers; for He said they should be hated of all men for His name's sake. If we had ceased to be persecuted and hated we might fear; but the prospect is encouraging.—J. of D., Vol. VII., p. 42.

When I hear persons say that they ought to occupy a station more exalted, than they do, and hide the talents they are in possession of, they have not the true wisdom they ought to have. There is a lack in them, or they would improve upon the talents given.—J. of D., Vol. VII., p. 162.

Take a course to let the Spirit of God leave your hearts, and every soul of you would apostatize.—J. of D., Vol. VII., p. 55.

Truth is obeyed when it is loved. Strict obedience to the truth will alone enable people to dwell in the presence of the Almighty.—J. of D., Vol. VII., p. 55.

When men come into this Church merely through having their judgments convinced, they still must have the Spirit of God bearing witness to their spirits, or they will leave the Church, as sure as they are living beings. The Saints must become one, as Jesus said His disciples should be one. They must have the Spirit testifying to them of the truth, or the light that is in them will become darkness, and they will forsake this kingdom and their religion. I wished to bear this testimony.—J. of D., Vol. VII., p. 55.

There will not be so many people that will go into that awful place that burns with fire and brimstone, where they sink down, down, down to the bottom of the bottomless pit, as the Christians say,—not near so many as the Christian world would have go there. That gives me great joy, notwithstanding all the perils and persecution we have suffered through the wickedness of the wicked. Liars, sorcerers, whoremongers, adulterers, and those that love and make a lie, will be found on the outside of the walls of the city; but they will never get into the bottom of the bottomless pit. Who will go there and become angels of perdition and suffer the wrath of an offended God? Those who sin against the Holy Ghost.—J. of D., Vol. VII., p. 144.

The eloquence of angels never can convince any person that God lives, and makes truth the habitation of His throne, independent of that eloquence being clothed with the power of the Holy Ghost; in the absence of this, it would be a combinat on of useless sounds.—J. of D., Vol. I., p. 90.

Embrace a doctrine that will purge sin and iniquity from your hearts, and sanctify you before God, and you are right, no matter how others act.—J. of D., Vol. IV., p. 78.

Every time you kick "Mormonism," you kick it up stairs: you never kick it down stairs. The Lord Almighty so orders it.—J. of D., Vol. VII., p. 145.

If you want to see the principle of devilism to perfection. hunt among those who have once enjoyed the faith of the holy gospel and then forsaken their religion. We have the best and the worst.—J. of D., Vol. VII., p. 145.

Darkness and sin were permitted to come on this earth. Man partook of the forbidden fruit in accordance with a plan devised from eternity, that mankind might be brought in contact with the principles and powers of darkness, that they might know the bitter and the sweet, the good and the evil, and be able to discern between light and darkness, to enable them to receive light continually.—J. of D., Vol. VII., p, 158.

I will not say, as do many, that the more I learn the more I am satisfied that I know nothing; for the more I learn the more I discern an eternity of knowledge to improve upon.—J. of D., Vol. VII., p. 162.

This American continent will be Zion, for it is so spoken of by the prophets. Jerusalem will be rebuilt and will be the place of gathering, and the tribe of Judah will gather there; but this continent of America is the land of Zion.—J. of D., Vol. V., p. 4.

One-third part of the spirits that were prepared for this earth rebelled against Jesus Christ, and were cast down to the earth, and they have been opposed to him from that day to this, with Lucifer at their heard. He is their great General Lucifer, the Son of the Morning. He was once a brilliant and influential character in heaven, and we will know more about him hereafter.—J. of D., Vol. V., p. 55.

It is the man who works hard, who sweats over the rock, and goes to the canyons for lumber, that I count more worthy of good food and dress than I am.—J. of D., Vol. V., p. 99.

Chastisements are grievous when they are received; but if they are received in patience, they will work out salvation for those who cheerfully submit to them.—J. of D., Vol. V., p. 124.

Mourning for the righteous dead springs from the ignorance and weakness that are planted within the mortal tabernacle, the organization of this house for the spirit to dwell in. No matter what pain we suffer, no matter what we pass through, we cling to our mother earth, and dislike to have any of her children leave us. We love to keep together the social family relation that we bear one to another, and do not like to part with each other; but could we have knowledge and see into eternity, if we were perfectly free from the weakness, blindness and lethargy with which we are clothed in the flesh, we should have no disposition to weep or mourn. —J. of D., Vol. IV., p. 131.

First reform in your moral character and conduct one towards another, so that every man and woman will deal honestly and walk uprightly with one another, and extend the arm of charity and benevolence to each other, as necessity requires. Be moral and strictly honest in every point, before you ask God to reform your spirit.—J. of D., Vol. IV., p. 61.

If we could see our heavenly Father, we should see a being similar to our earthly parent, with this difference: our Father in heaven is exalted and glorified. He has received His thrones, His principalities and powers, and He sits as a governor, as a monarch, and overrules kingdoms, thrones and dominions that have been bequeathed to Him, and such as we anticipate receiving. While He was in the flesh, as we are, He was as we are.—J. of D., Vol. IV., p. 54.

When we have done with the flesh, and have departed to the spirit world, you will find that we are independent of those evil spirits. But while you are in the flesh you will suffer by them, and cannot control them, only by your faith in the name of Jesus Christ and by the keys of the eternal priesthood. When the spirit is unlocked from the tabernacle it is as free, pure, holy and independent of them as the sun is of this earth.—J. of D. Vol. IV., p. 134.

The spirit of every man and woman that gets into the celestial kingdom must overcome the flesh, must war against the flesh until the seeds of sin that are sown in the flesh are brought into subjection to the law of Christ.—J. of D., Vol. IV., p, 197.

Natural philosophy is the plan of salvation, and the plan of salvation is natural philosophy.—J. of D. Vol. IV., p. 203.

There is no spirit but what was pure and holy when it came here from the celestial world. There is no spirit among the human family that was begotten in hell ; none that were begotten by angles, or by any inferior being. They were not produced by any being less than our Father in heaven. He is the Father of our spirits, and if we could know, understand and do His will, every soul would be prepared to return back into His presence. And when they get there, they would see that they had formerly lived there for ages ; that they had previously been acquainted with every nook and corner, with the palaces, walks and gardens ; and they would embrace their Father, and He would embrace them.—J. of D., Vol. IV., p. 268.

The kingdom of our God that is set upon the earth, does not require men of many words and flaming oratorical talents, to establish truth and righteousness. It is not the many words that accomplish the designs of our Father in heaven; with Him it is the acts of the people more than their words.—J. of D., Vol. IV., p. 20.

We are placed on this earth to prove whether we are worthy to go into the celestial world, the terrestrial or the telestial, or to hell.—J. of D., Vol. IV., p. 269.

Serve God according to the best knowledge you have, and lie down and sleep quietly ; and when the devil comes along and says, "You are not a very good Saint, you might enjoy greater blessings and more of the power of God, and have the vision of your mind opened, if you would live up to your privileges, tell him to leave ; that you have long ago forsaken his ranks and enlisted in the army of Jesus, who is your captain, and that you want no more of the devil.—J. of D., Vol. IV., p. 270.

The spirit of truth will do more to bring persons to light and knowledge than flowery words.—J. of D., Vol. IV., p. 21.

Many people are unwilling to do one thing for themselves in case of sickness, but ask God to do it all.—J. of D., Vol. IV., p. 25.

I would rather be chopped to pieces at night, and resurrected in the morning each day throughout a period of three score years and ten, than be deprived of speaking freely, or be afraid of doing so.—J. of D., Vol. I., p. 364.

A man never can be a polished scoundrel, until he can figure in polished society. It proves the truth of the saying, that it takes all the revelations of God, and every good principle in the world to make a man perfectly ripe for hell.—J. of D., Vol. I., p. 362.

Let the past experience be buried in the land of forgetfulness, if the Lord will; but if this is done at all, it will be by showing kindness towards us in the future. If they wish us to forget the past, let them cease to make and circulate falsehoods about us, and let all the good people of the Government say,—"*Let us do this people good for the future, and not try to crush them down all the day long by continuing to persecute them.*"

If we are here by chance, if we happened to slip into this world from nothing, we shall soon slip out of this world to nothing, hence nothing will remain.—J. of D., Vol. IV., p. 60.

The devil is just as much opposed to Jesus now as he was when the revolt took place in heaven. And as the devil increases his numbers by getting the people to be wicked, so Jesus Christ increases His numbers and strength by getting the people to be humble and righteous. The human family are going to the polls by and by, and they wish to know which party is going to carry the day.—J. of D., Vol. IV., p. 38.

If we are a company of poor, ignorant, deluded creatures, why do they not show us a better example?—J. of D., Vol. I., p. 365.

If children have sinned against their parents, or husbands against their wives, or wives against their husbands, let them confess their faults one to another and forgive each other, and there let the confession stop; and then let them ask pardon from their God. Confess your sins to whoever you have sinned against, and let it stop there.

If you have committdd a sin against the community, confess to them. If you have sinned in your family, confess there.

Confess your sins, iniquities and follies where that confession belongs, and learn to classify your actions.—J. of D., Vol. IV., p. 79.

Nothing less than the privilege of increasing eternally, in every sense of the word, can satisfy the immortal spirit. If the endless stream of knowledge from the eternal fountain could all be drunk in by organized intelligence, so sure immortality would come to an end, and all eternity be thrown upon the retrograde path.—J. of D., Vol. I., p. 350.

God is our Father, and Jesus Christ is our elder brother, and both are our everlasting friends.—J. of D., Vol. VII., p. 193.

The only true believers are they who *prove their belief* by their obedience to the requirements of the gospel.—J. of D., Vol. I., p. 234.

A flock of sheep consisting of thousands must be clean indeed if some of them are not smutty.—J. of D., Vol. I., p. 213.

The gospel of salvation is perfectly calculated to cause division. It strikes at the root of the very existence of mankind in their wickedness, evil designs, passions and wicked calculations. There is no evil among the human family, but at the foundation of which it strikes effectually, and comes in contact with every evil passion that rises in the heart of man. It is opposed to every evil practice of men, and consequently it disturbs them in the wicked courses they are pursuing.—J. of D., Vol. I., p. 235.

The God Mr. Baptist believes in is without body, parts or passions. The God that his "brother Mormon" believes in is described in the Bible as being a personage of tabernacle, having eyes to see, for he that made the eye shall he not see? Having ears to hear, for his ears are open to hear the prayers of the righteous. He has limbs that He can walk, for the Lord God walked in the garden in the cool of the day. He conversed with His children, as in the case of Moses at the fiery bush, and with Abraham on the plains of Mamre. He also ate and drank with Abraham and others. That is, the God the Mormons believe in, but their very religious Christian brethren do not believe in the God of Abraham, Isaac and Jacob, which is the God the Bible sets forth, as an organized corporeal being.—J. of D., Vol. I., p. 238.

21

It is a mistaken idea to suppose that others can prevent me from enjoying the light of God in my soul; all hell cannot hinder me from enjoying Zion in my own heart, if my individual will yields obedience to the requirements and mandates of my heavenly Master.—J. of D., Vol. I., p. 311.

Children have all confidence in their mothers; and if mothers would take proper pains, they can instill into the hearts of their children what they please. You will, no doubt, recollect reading, in the Book of Mormon, of two thousand young men, who were brought up to believe that, if they put their whole trust in God, and served Him no power would overcome them. You also recollect reading of them going out to fight, and so bold were they, and so mighty their faith, that it was impossible for their enemies to slay them. This power and faith they obtained through the teachings of their mothers.—J. of D., Vol. I., p. 67.

That moment that men seek to build up themselves, in preference to the kingdom of God, and seek to hoard up riches, while the widow and the fatherless, the sick and afflicted around them are in poverty and want, it proves that their hearts are weaned from their God.—J. of D., Vol. I., p. 273.

It is as much as we can do to keep the Christians of the nineteenth century from cutting our throats because we differ from them in our religious belief.—J. of D., Vol. VII., p. 165.

If I could not master my mouth, I would my knees, and make them bend until my mouth would speak.—J. of D., Vol. VII., p. 164.

All who live according to the best principles in their possession, or that they can understand, will receive peace, glory, comfort, joy, and a crown that will be far beyond what they are anticipating. They will not be lost.—J. of D., Vol. VII., p. 192.

I will not ask any person to embrace anything that is not in the New Testament until they have asked God if it is true or untrue, who will satisfy them if they ask in faith nothing doubting.—J. of D., Vol. I., p. 244.

Do not seek for that which you cannot magnify, but practice upon that which you have in your possession.—J. of D., Vol. VII., p. 239.

It would be as easy for a gnat to trace the history of man back to his origin as for man to fathom the first cause of all things, lift the veil of eternity, and reveal the mysteries that have been sought after by philosophers from the beginning. What, then, should be the calling and duty of the children of men? Instead of inquiring after the origin of the Gods—instead of trying to explore the depths of eternities that have been, that are, and that will be—instead of endeavoring to discover the boundaries of boundless space, let them seek to know the object of their present existence, and how to apply, in the most profitable manner for their mutual good and salvation, the intelligence they possess.—J. of D., Vol. VII., p. 284.

The being whom we call Father was the father of the spirit of the Lord Jesus Christ, and He was also His father pertaining to the flesh. Infidels and Christians, make all you can of this statement. The Bible, which all Christians profess to believe, reveals that fact, and it reveals the truth upon that point, and I am a witness of its truth. The apostles who were personally acquainted with Jesus Christ did know and understand what they wrote, and they wrote the truth.—J. of D., Vol. VII., p. 286.

When the spirit leaves the body it goes into the spirit world, where the spirits of men are classified according to their own wills or pleasure, as men are here, only they are in a more pure and refined state of existence.—J. of D., Vol. VII., p. 288.

Salvation is an individual operation. I am the only person that can possibly save myself.—J. of D., Vol. I., p. 312.

There is *not a truth on earth or in heaven that is not embraced in Mormonism.*—J. of D., Vol. I., p. 244.

I am here to testify to hundreds of instances of men, women and children being healed by the power of God through the laying on of hands: and many I have seen raised from the gates of death, and brought back from the verge of eternity; and some whose spirits had actually left their bodies, returned again. I testify that I have seen the sick healed by the laying on of hands, according to the promise of the Savior.—J. of D., Vol. I., p. 240.

There never was a time when there were not Gods and worlds, and when men were not passing through the same ordeals that we are now passing through. That course has been from all eternity and it is and will be to all eternity.—J. of D , Vol. VII., p. 333.

When you tell me that Father Adam was made as we make adobies, from the earth, you tell me what I deem an idle tale. When you tell me that the beasts of the field were produced in that manner, you are speaking idle words, devoid of meaning. There is no such thing in all the eternities where the Gods dwell; mankind are here because they are the offspring of parents who were first brought here from another planet, and power was given them to propagate their species, and they were commanded to multiply and replenish the earth.—J. of D., Vol. VII., p. 285.

We will round up our shoulders and bear up the ponderous weight, carry the gospel to the uttermost parts of the earth, gather Israel, redeem Zion and continue our operations until we bind Satan, and the kingdoms of this world become the kingdom of our Lord and His Christ, and no power can hinder it.—J. of D., Vol. I., p. 189.

The "Mormon" Elders will tell you that all people must receive this gospel—the gospel of Jesus Christ, and be baptized for the remission of sins, or they cannot be saved.   Let me explain this to you.   They cannot go where God and Christ dwell, for that is a kingdom of itself—the celestial kingdom.   Jesus said, "In my Father's house are many mansions," or kingdoms.   They will come forth in the first, second or some other resurrection, if they have not been guilty of the particular sins I have just mentioned; and they will enjoy a kingdom and a glory greater than they had ever anticipated.   When we talk about people's being damned, I would like to have all understand that we do not use the term "damnation" in the sense that it is used by the sectarian world.   Universal salvation or redemption is the doctrine of the Bible; but the people do not know how or where to discriminate between truth and error.   All those who have done according to the best of their knowledge, whether they are Christians, Pagans, Jews, Mohammedans, or any other class of men that have ever lived upon the earth, that have dealt honestly and justly with their fellow beings, walked uprightly before each other, loved mercy, tried to put down iniquity, and done as far right as they knew how, according to the laws they lived under, no matter what the laws were, will share in a resurrection that will be glorious far beyond the conception of mortals.—J. of D., Vol. VII., p. 288.

. Do you not know that the possession of your property is like a shadow, or the dew of the morning before the noonday sun, that you cannot have any assurance of its control for a single moment? It is the unseen hand of Providence that controls it.—J. of D. Vol. I., p. 114.

No person can be a saint, unless he receives the holy gospel, for the purity, justice, holiness, and eternal duration of it.—J. of D. Vol. I., p. 114.

I will do the work the Lord has appointed unto me. You do the same and fear not, for the Lord manages the helm of the ship of Zion ; and on any other ship I do not wish to be. —J. of D., Vol. I., p. 189.

How often to all human appearance, has this kingdom been blotted out from the earth, but the Lord has put His hand over the people, and it has passed through and come out two, three and four times larger than before. Our enemies have kicked us, and cuffed us, and driven us from pillar to post, and we have multiplied and increased the more, until we have become what we are this day.—J. of D., Vol. I., p. 191.

The devil has put the whole world on the watch against us. It is impossible for us to make the least move without exciting, if not all the world, at least a considerable portion of it. They are excited at what we do, and strange to relate, they are no less excited at what we do not do.—J. of D., Vol. I., p. 189.

Do you suppose that this people will ever see the day that they will rest in perfect security, in hopes of becoming like another people, nation, state, kingdom or society? *They never will.* Christ and Satan never can be friends. Light and darkness will always remain opposites.—J. of D., Vol. I., p. 188.

When evil is present with us, we must overcome it, or be overcome by it. When the devil is in our hearts, tempting us to do that which is wrong, we must resist him, or be led captive by him.—J. of D., Vol, I., p. 92.

The speculation I am after, is to exchange this world, which, in its present state, passes away, for a world that is eternal and unchangeable, for a glorified world filled with eternal riches, for the world that is made an inheritance for the Gods of eternity.—J. of D., Vol. I., p. 327.

Do the righteous of this people cause persecution to come upon themselves? No. Do the principles of the gospel create prejudice and persecution against them? No. But it is the disposition of the wicked to oppose the principles of truth and righteousness which causes it.—J. of D., Vol. I. p. 186.

To saint and sinner, believer and unbeliever, I wish here to offer one word of advice and counsel by revealing the mystery that abides with this people called Latter-day Saints ; it is the Spirit of the living God that leads them ; it is the Spirit of the Almighty that binds them together ; it is the influence of the Holy Ghost that makes them love each other like little children ; it is the Spirit of Jesus Christ that makes them willing to lay down their lives for the cause of truth, and it was that same Spirit that caused Joseph, our martyred prophet to lay down his life for the testimony of what the Lord revealed to him.—J. of D., Vol. I., p. 145.

I have nothing to fear in all the persecutions or hardships I may pass through in connection with this people, but the one thing, and that is to stray from the religion I have embraced and be forsaken by my God. If you or I should see that day, we shall see at once that the world will love its own; and affliction, persecution, death, fire and the sword will cease to follow us.—J. of D., Vol. I., p. 144.

Money is not real capital, it bears the title only. True capital is labor and is confined to the laboring classes. They only possess it. It is the bone, sinew, nerve and muscle of man that subdue the earth, make it yield its strength and administer to his varied wants. This power tears down mountains and fills up valleys, builds cities and temples, and paves the streets. In short what is there that yields shelter and comfort to civilized man that is not produced by the strength of his arm making the elements bend to his will.—J. of D., Vol. I., p. 254.

Though the enemy had power to kill our *prophet*, that is, *kill his body*, did *he* not accomplish all that was in *his heart* to accomplish in *his day*? He did to my certain knowledge, and I have many witnesses here that heard him declare that he had done everything he could do—he had revealed everything that could be revealed at *present*, he had prepared the way for the people to walk in, and no man or woman should be deprived of going into the presence of the Father and the Son and enjoying an eternal exaltation if they would *walk in the path he had pointed out.*—J. of D., Vol. I., p. 132.

So long as you are able to walk and attend to your business, it is folly to say that you need ardent spirits to keep you alive. The constitution that a person has should be nourished and cherished ; and whenever we take anything into the system to force and stimulate it beyond its natural capacity, it shortens life. I am physician enough to know that. When you are tired and think you need a little spirituous liquor, take some bread and butter, or bread and milk, and lie down and rest. Do not labor so hard as to deem it requisite to get half drunk in order to keep up your spirits. If you will follow this counsel, you will be full of life and health, and will increase your intelligence, your joy and comfort.—J. of D., Vol. VII., p. 337.

All I desire to live for is to see the inhabitants of the earth acknowledge God, bow down to Him, and confess His supremacy, and His righteous covenant. To Him let every knee bow, and every tongue confess, and let all creation say Amen to His wise providences. Let every person declare His allegiance to God, and then live to it, saying, "As for me and my house we will serve the Lord. *As for me, and all I have, it is the Lord's, and shall be dedicated to Him all my days.*" If this can be done, happiness is here, angels are here, God is here and we are wrapped in the visions of eternity.—J. of D., Vol. I., p. 94.

The principle opposite to that of eternal increase from the beginning, leads down to hell ; the person decreases, loses his knowledge, tact, talent and ultimately, in a short period of time is lost ; he returns to his mother earth, his name is forgotten. But where, O ! where is his spirit? I will not now take the time to follow his destiny ; but here strong language *could* be used, for when the Lord Jesus Christ shall be revealed after the termination of the thousand years' rest, He will summon the armies of heaven for the conflict, He will come forth in flaming fire, He will descend to execute the mandates of an incensed God, and amid the thunderings of the wrath of Omnipotence, roll up the heavens as a scroll and destroy death and him that has the power of it. The rebellious will be thrown back into their native element, there to remain myriads of years before their dust will again be revived, before they will be reorganized. Some might argue that this principle would lead to the reorganization of Satan, and all the devils. I say nothing about this only what the Lord says, that when " He comes He will destroy *death* and him that has the power of it." It cannot be annihilated; you cannot annihilate matter. If you could it would prove there was empty space. If philosophers could annihilate the least conceivable amount of matter, they could then prove there was the minutest vacuum, or *empty space* but there is not even that much, and it is beyond the power of man to prove that there is *any.*—J. of D., Vol. I., p. 118.

Because of the weakness of human nature, it must crumble to the dust. But in all the revolutions and changes in the existence of men, in the eternal world which they inhabit, and in the knowledge they have obtained as people on the earth, there is no such thing as principle, power, wisdom, knowledge, life, position or anything that can be imagined, that remains stationary—they must increase or decrease.— J. of D., Vol. I., p. 350.

Men should act upon the principle of righteousness because it is right, and is a principle which they love to cherish and see practiced by all men. They should love mercy because of its benevolence, charity, love, clemency and of all of its lovely attributes, and be inspired thereby to deal justly, fairly, honorably, meting out to others their just deservings.—J. of D., Vol. I., p. 119.

Practical religion is what we all need to prepare us to enjoy that which we have in our anticipations—that which we hold in our faith. Merely the theory of any religion does people but little good. This is the great failing of Bible Christians, as they are called. They have the theory of the religion of which the Bible testifies, but the practical part they spurn from them.—J. of D., Vol. IV., p. 341.

All those who wish to possess true riches, desire the riches that will endure. Then look at the subject of salvation where you will find true riches. They are to be found in the principles of the gospel of salvation, and are not to be found anywhere else.—J. of D., Vol. I., p. 269.

Suppose we say there was once a beginning to all things, then we must conclude there will undoubtedly be an end. Can eternity be circumscribed? If it can, there is an end of all wisdom, knowledge, power and glory—all will sink into eternal annihilation.—J. of D., Vol. I., p. 353.

Which would produce the greatest good to man, to give him his agency and draw a vail over him, or to give him certain blessings and privileges, let him live in a certain degree of light, and enjoy a certain glory, and take his agency from him, compelling him to remain in that position, without any possible chance of progress? I say the greatest good that could be produced by the all-wise Conductor of the universe to His creature, man, was to do just as He has done.—J. of D., Vol. I., p. 351.

The Lord does not thank you for your alms, long prayers, sanctimonious speeches and long faces, if you refuse to extend the hand of benevolence and charity to your fellow creatures, and lift them up, and encourage and strengthen the feeble, while they are contending against the current of mortal ills.—J. of D., Vol. I., p. 245.

The Holy Ghost takes of the Father and of the Son and shows it to the disciples. It shows them things past, present and to come. It opens the vision of the mind, unlocks the treasures of wisdom, and they begin to understand the things of God ; their minds are exalted on high ; their conceptions of God and His creations are dignified, and "Hallelujah to God and the Lamb in the highest," is the constant language of their hearts. They comprehend themselves and the great object of their existence. They also comprehend the designs of the wicked ones, and the designs of those who serve him; they comprehend the designs of the Almighty in forming the earth and mankind upon it, and the ultimate purpose of all His creations. It leads them to drink at the fountain of eternal wisdom, justice and truth ; they grow in grace and in the knowledge of the truth as it is in Jesus Christ until they see as they are seen, and know as they are known.—J. of D., Vol. I., p. 241.

The character of a person is formed through life, to a greater or less extent, by the teachings of the mother. The traits of early impressions that she gives the child, will be characteristic points in his character through every avenue of his mortal existence.—J. of D., Vol. I., p. 67.

It is necessary that we should be tried, tempted and buffeted to make us feel the weakness of this mortal flesh.—J. of D., Vol. I., p. 359.

Directly behind a frowning Providence oftentimes are concealed the greatest blessings that mankind can desire.—J. of D., Vol. I., p. 198.

I am at the defiance of the rulers of the greatest nation on the earth, with the United States all put together, to produce a more loyal people than the Latter-day Saints.—J. of D., Vol. 1., p. 361.

All there is of any worth or value in the world is incorporated in our glorious religion, and designed to exalt the minds of the children of men to a permanent, celestial and eternal station.—J. of D., Vol. I., p. 341.

I may have thousands of wealth locked up today, and hold checks for immense sums on the best banking institutions in the world, but have I any surety that I shall be worth a cent tomorrow morning? Not the least. The Lord Almighty can send fire and destruction when He pleases, destroying towns and swallowing up cities in the bellowing earthquake. He can set up kingdoms and make communities wealthy, and bring them to poverty at His pleasure. When He pleases, He can give them wealth, comfort and ease, and on the other hand torment them with poverty, distress and sore afflictions. Who can realize this? All the world ought, and especially the Saints.—J. of D., Vol. I., p. 340.

The Lord Almighty can do His own work and no power of man can stay the potency of His wonder-working hand. Men may presume to dictate to the Lord; they come to naught, but His work moves steadily forward.—J. of D., Vol. I., p. 198.

When I cannot feed myself through the means God has placed in my power, it is then time enough for Him to exercise His providence in an unusual manner to administer to my wants. But while we can help ourselves, it is our duty to do so. If a saint of God be locked up in prison, by his enemies, to starve to death, it is then time enough for God to interpose, and feed him.—J. of D., Vol. I., p. 108.

It has been, and is now, believed by numerous individuals, that the brute creation, by increase in knowledge and wisdom, change their physical or bodily organization, through numerous states of existence, so that the minutest insect, in lapse of time, can take to itself the human form, and *visa versa*. This is one of the most inconsistent ideas that could be possibly entertained in the mind of man; it is called the transmigration of souls. It is enough for me to know that mankind are made to improve themselves. All creation, visible and invisible, is the workmanship of our God, the Supreme Architect and Ruler of the whole, who organized the world, and created every living thing upon it, to act in its sphere and order. To this end has He ordained all things to increase and multiply. The Lord God Almighty has decreed this principle to be the great governing law of existence, and for that purpose are we formed. Furthermore, if man can understand and receive it, mankind are organized to receive intelligence until they become perfect in the sphere they are appointed to fill, which is far ahead of us at present. When we use the term perfection. it applies to man in his present condition, as well as to heavenly beings. We are now, or may be, as perfect in *our sphere* as God and angels are in theirs, but the greatest intelligence in existence can continually ascend to greater heights of perfection.—J. of D., Vol. I., p. 92.

We read in the Bible, that there is one glory of the sun, another glory of the moon, and another glory of the stars. In the Book of Doctrine and Covenants these glories are called telestial, terrestrial, and celestial, which is the highest. These are worlds, different departments, or mansions, in our Father's house. Now those men, or those women, who know no more about the power of God, and the influences of the Holy Spirit, than to be led entirely by another person, suspending their own understanding, and pinning their faith upon another's sleeve, will never be capable of entering into the celestial glory, to be crowned as they anticipate; they will never be capable of becoming Gods. They cannot rule themselves, to say nothing of ruling others, but they must be dictated to in every trifle, like a child. They cannot control themselves in the least, but James, Peter, or somebody else must control them. They never can become Gods, nor be crowned as rulers with glory, immortality, and eternal lives. They never can hold sceptres of glory, majesty, and power in the celestial kingdom. Who will? Those who are valient and inspired with the true independence of heaven, who will go forth boldly in the service of their God, leaving others to do as they please, determined to do right, though all mankind besides should take the opposite course. Will this apply to any of you? Your own hearts can answer.—J. of D., Vol. I., p. 312.

Suppose the devil does tempt you, must you of necessity enter into partnership again with him, open your doors, and bid him welcome to your house, and tell him to reign there? Why do you not reflect, and tell master devil, with all his associates and imps, to be gone, feeling you have served him long enough.—J. of D., Vol. I., p. 323.

If true principles are revealed from heaven to men, and if there are angels, and there is a possibility of their communicating to the human family, always look for an opposite power, an evil power, to give manifestations also; look out for the counterfeit.—J. of D., Vol. VII., p. 240.

When death is passed, the power of Satan has no more influence over a faithful individual; that spirit is free, and can command the power of Satan. The penalty demanded by the fall has been fully paid; all is accomplished pertaining to it, when the tabernacle of a faithful person is returned to earth. All that was lost is passed away, and that person will again receive his body. When he is in the spirit world, he is free from those contaminating and condemning influences of Satan that we are now subject to. Here our bodies are subject to being killed by our enemies—our names to being cast out as evil. We are prosecuted, hated, not beloved; though I presume that we are as much beloved here as the spirits of the saints are in the spirit world by those spirits who hate righteousness. It is the same warfare, but we will have power over them. Those who have passed through the vail have power over the evil spirits to command, and they must obey.— J. of D., Vol. VII., p. 240.

Oppression, persecution, afflictions, and other trials and privations are necessary as a test to all professing to be Saints, that they may have an opportunity to witness the workings of the power which is opposed to truth and holiness.—J. of D., Vol. VII., p. 242.

Let the spirit that comes from the eternal world, which at the outset is pure and holy, with the influence God gives to it, master all the passions of the body, and bring it under subjection to the will of Christ. That course makes us Saints.— J. of D., Vol. VII., p. 243.

Whether a truth be found with professed infidels, or with Universalists, or the Church of Rome, or the Methodists, the Church of England, the Presbyterians, the Baptists, the Quakers, the Shakers, or any other of the various and numerous different sects and parties, all of whom have more or less truth, it is the business of the Elders of this Church (Jesus, their elder brother, being at their head,) to gather up all the truths in the world pertaining to life and salvation, to the gospel we preach, to mechanism of every kind, to the sciences, and to philosophy, wherever it may be found in every nation, kindred, tongue, and people, and bring it to Zion. The people upon this earth have a great many errors, and they have also a great many truths. This statement is not only true of the nations termed civilized—those who profess to worship the true God, but is equally applicable to pagans of all countries, for in their religious rites and ceremonies may be found a great many truths which we will also gather home to Zion. All truth is for the salvation of the children of men—for their benefit and learning—for their furtherance in the principles of divine knowledge.—J. of D., Vol. VII., p. 283.

The Latter-day Saints understand the Bible as it reads, but the generality of modern Christians disagree with us, and say it needs interpreting. They cannot believe our Lord means what He says in the 16th chapter of Mark, when He tells His Apostles to "go into all the world, and preach the gospel to every creature. He that believeth and is baptized shall be saved; but he that believeth not shall be damned. And these signs shall follow them that believe," etc. "Now," say they, "we cannot believe that as it is written, but we have a very pretty interpretation which suits us much better than the plain text. And furthermore we have a sweeping argument that will destroy all your system from beginning to end, and prove there is to be no more revelation." Let us look at the passage here referred to. John, while upon the Isle of Patmos, had a revelation which he wrote, and he concluded the same by saying, "For I testify unto every man that heareth the words of the prophecy of this book, if any man shall add unto these things, God shall add unto him the plagues that are written in this book; and if any man shall take away from the words of the book of this prophecy, God shall take away His part out of the book of life, and out of the holy city, and from the things which are written in this book." When this book, the Bible, was compiled, it was selected by the council of Carthage from a pile of books more than this pulpit could hold, which has been printed, and bound in almost all shapes and sizes, and called the Bible. John's revelation was one of the many books destined by that council to form the Bible. And the saying which we have quoted, and which constitutes the sweeping argument of modern Christians against new revelation, only alludes to this particular book, which was to be kept sacred, as the word of the Lord to John, and not to the whole Bible; nor does it prohibit the Saints in his day, or the Saints in any future time, from getting new revelation for themselves. That is not all; if we turn to the writings of Moses, we find the same sentiment, and almost the same language used. Moses says, "Ye shall not add unto the word which I command you, neither shall ye diminish ought from it, that ye may keep the commandments of the Lord your God which I command you." So if such quotations are given with the intent to' shut the heavens, and put an end to all new revelation, then the revelations given to prophets who arose after Moses, and the revelations given to Jesus Christ and His Apostles, including John and his revelation on the Isle of Patmos, all amount to nothing, and are not worthy of our notice. This "sweeping argument," when it is examined, sweeps away rather too much; besides, John's gospel and his epistle to his bretheren were written after he wrote his revelation on the Isle of Patmos; consequently he would destroy his own system; but it sets forth the ignorance and short-sightedness of those who have not the testimony of Jesus, which is the spirit of prophecy.—J. of D. Vol. I., p. 242.

Let us dedicate ourselves, our families, our substance, our time, our talents, and everything we have upon the face of this world, with all that will hereafter be entrusted to us, to the Lord our God; let the whole be devoted to the building up of His kingdom upon the earth.—J. of. D. Vol. I., p. 200.

Teach your families how to control themselves; teach them good and wholesome doctrine, and 'practice the same in your own lives. This is the place for you to become polished shafts in the quiver of the Almighty.—J. of D. Vol. I., p. 47.

When a man is capable of correcting you, and of giving you light, and true doctrine, do not get up an altercation, but submit to be taught like little children, and strive with all your might to understand.—J. of D. Vol. I., p. 47.

Bancroft Library

We believe the New Testament, and consequenly, to be consistent, we must believe in new revelation, visions, angels, in all the gifts of the Holy Ghost, and all the promises contained in these books, and believe it about as it reads.—J. of D. Vol. I., p. 242.]

The Millennium consists in this—every heart in the Church and kingdom of God being united in one; the kingdom increasing to the overcoming of everything opposed to the economy of heaven, and Satan being bound, and having a seal set upon him. All things else will be as they are now, we shall eat, drink, and wear clothing. Let the people be holy, and the earth under their feet will be holy. Let the people be holy and filled with the Spirit of God, and every animal and creeping thing will be filled with peace; the soil of the earth will bring forth in its strength, and the fruits thereof will be meat for man. The more purity that exists, the less is the strife; the more kind we are to our animals, the more will peace increase, and the savage nature of the brute creation vanish away. If the people will not serve the devil another moment whilst they live, if this congregation is possessed of that spirit and resolution, here in this house is the Millennium. Let the inhabitants of this city be possessed of that spirit, let the people of the territory be possessed of that spirit, and here is the Millennium. Let the whole people of the United States be possessed of that spirit, and here is the Millennium, and so will it spread over all the world.—J. of D. Vol. I., p. 203.

The power which belongs to the true riches is gained by pursuing a righteous course, by maintaining an upright deportment towards all men, and especially towards the household of faith, yielding to each other, giving freely of that which the Lord has given to you, thus you can secure to yourselves eternal riches; and gain influence and power over all your friends, as well as your enemies.—J. of D., Vol. I. p. 273.

Were I to say to a son, The whole earth is in my hands to dispose of as I will: I can make you the sovereign of the universe—the possessor of the gold, the silver, the mountains, the valleys, the rivers, the lakes the seas, and all that float upon them and that live upon the face of the whole earth; for it is mine to give to you, my son, if you will serve me one month faithfully; I require nothing of you that will give you the least pain! all I require is strict obedience to my law. My son faithfully serves me during twenty-nine days, and on the thirtieth day, for the value of a straw, or for a mess of pottage he sells his right and title to all I had promised him. This comparison falls very far short of showing the loss a Saint sustains when he turns away from his God and his religion.—J. of D., Vol. VII., p. 133.

As long as the spirit and body hold together, my tongue shall be swift against evil, the Lord Almighty being my helper. Though it may be in " Mormon" Elders, among the people in or out of the Church, if they come in my path where I can chastize them, the Lord Almighty being my helper, my tongue shall be swift against evil ; and if evil come, let it come. If for this my body shall fall, let it fall ; when they have destroyed the body, then they have no more that they can do ; that is the end of their power, and of the power of the devil on this earth ; but Jesus Christ has power to destroy both soul and body in hell.—J. of D., Vol. I., p. 42.

Were I to make war upon an innocent people, because I had the power to possess myself of their territory, their silver, gold, and other property, and be the cause of slaying, say fifty thousand strong, hale, hearty men, and devolving consequent suffering upon one hundred thousand women and children, who would suffer through privation and want, I am very much more guilty of murder than is the man who kills only one person to obtain his pocket-book.—J. of D., Vol. VII, p. 137.

There is one virtue, attribute, or principle, which, if cherished and practiced by the Saints, would prove salvation to thousands upon thousands. I allude to charity, or love, from which proceed 'forgiveness, long suffering, kindness, and patience.—J. of D., Vol. VII., p. 133.

If a man drinks at the fountain of eternal life, he is as happy under the broad canopy of heaven, without a home, as in a palace. This I know by experience. I know that the things of this world, from beginning to end, from the possession of mountains of gold down to a crust of johnycake, makes little or no difference in the happiness of an individual. The things of this world add to our natural comfort, and are necessary to sustain mortal life. We need these comforts to preserve our earthly existence; and many suppose, when they have them in great abundance, that they have all that is needed to make them happy. They are striving continually, and with all their might, for that which does not add one particle to their happiness, though it may not add to their comfort, and perhaps to the length of their lives, if they do not kill themselves in their eagerness to grasp the gilded butterfly. But those things have nothing to do with the spirit, feeling, consolation, light, glory, peace, and joy that pertain to heaven and heavenly things, which is the food of the everlasting spirit within us.—J. of D., Vol. VII, p. 135.

Do not be so full of religion as to look upon every little overt act that others may commit as being the unpardonable sin that will place them beyond the reach of redemption and the favors of our God.—J. of D., Vol. VII, p. 136.

Our religion teaches us truth, virtue, holiness, faith in God and in His Son Jesus Christ. It reveals mysteries; it brings to mind things past and present—unfolding clearly things to come. It is the foundation of mechanism; it is the spirit that gives intelligence to every living being upon the earth. All true philosophy originates from that fountain from which we draw wisdom, knowledge, truth, and power. What does it teach us? To love God and our fellow creatures, to be compassionate, full of mercy, long-suffering and patient to the froward and to those who are ignorant. There is glory in our religion that no other religion that has ever been established upon the earth, in the absence of the true Priesthood, ever posessed. It is the fountain of all intelligence; it is to bring heaven to earth and exalt earth to heaven, to prepare all intelligence that God has placed in the hearts of the children of men to mingle with that intelligence which dwells in eternity, and to elevate the mind above the trifling and frivolous objects of time, which tend downward to destruction. It frees the mind of man from darkness and ignorence, gives him that intelligence that flows from heaven, and qualifies him to comprehend all things. This is the character of the religion we believe in.—J. of D. Vol. VII., p. 140.

I say *shame* on that man who will give way to his passions and use the name of God or of Christ to curse his ox or his horse, or any creature which God has made ; it is a disgrace to him.—J. of D., Vol. I., p. 241.

That a man is willing to die for his religion is no proof of its being true; neither is it proof that a religion is false when one of its votaries apostatizes from it.—J. of D., Vol. VII, p. 140.

I may heap up gold and silver like the mountains; I may gather around me property, goods and chattels, but I could have no glory in that compared with my religion ; it is the fountain of light and intelligence ; it swallows up the truth contained in all the philosophy of the world, both heathen and Christian ; it circumscribes the wisdom of man ; it circumscribes all the wisdom and power of the world; it reaches to that within the veil. Its bounds, its circumference, its end, its height and depth are beyond the comprehension of mortals, *for it has none.*—J. of D., Vol. I., p. 39.

If you have gold and silver, let it not come between you and your duty.—J. of D. Vol. I., p. 202.

When the breath leaves the body, your life has not become extinct; your life is still in existance. And when you are in the spirit world, everything there will appear as natural as things now do. Spirits will be familiar with spirits in the spirit world—will converse, behold, and exercise every variety of communication one with another as familiarly and naturally as while here in tabernacles.—J. of D., Vol. VII., p. 239.

If we are faithful to our religion, when we go into the spirit world, the fallen spirits—Lucifer and the third part of the heavenly hosts that came with him, and the spirits of wicked men who have dwelt upon this earth, the whole of them combined will have no influence over our spirits.—J. of D., Vol. VII., p. 240.

The thrones and kingdoms of earth are frequently changing hands. Adventurers rise up or go forth and establish new governments, and in a few short years they are cast down to give place to more successful powers. All earthly things are changing hands. The gold, the silver, and other property pass from my hands to yours, and from yours to the hands of others. Shame on a people that place their affections upon this changing matter! Love God and the things that change not.—J. of D., Vol. VII., p. 337.

The child who has his father's razor, or any other article dangerous for him to handle, and about the use of which he has no knowledge, when deprived of it, his trials are equal to ours, according to his capacity. We seldom think of the trials of our little ones when we say to them, you must not have this or that; you must do so and so to receive my smiles and approbation; you must not think for a moment that your judgment, wisdom, experience, and wishes are to be compared with mine. Does not the Father of all living conduct Himself in this wise towards His children? He has revealed to us that He will prepare us for glory, for life eternal,—will preserve our identity forever, if we will be guided by him. But we must be obedient to him, for He understands more than we do. We should destroy ourselves if we were suffered to take our own way; hence we are taught to suffer the Father to point out our path to an eternal duration hereafter, where our present afflictions will appear as flimsy as the shadows of the morning that flee upon the approach of day.—J. of D., Vol. VII., p. 275.

If a man is worth millions of bushels of wheat and corn, he is not wealthy enough to suffer his servant girl to sweep a single kernel of it into the fire; let it be eaten by something, and pass again into the earth, and thus fulfill the purpos for which it grew.—J. of D. Vol. I., p. 253.

The man who lays up his gold and silver, who caches it away in a bank, or in his iron safe, or buries it up in the earth, and comes here, and professes to be a Saint, would tie up the hands of every indivdual in this kingdom, and make them his servants if he could.—J. of D., Vol. I., p. 253.

If I am not smart enough to take care of what the Lord lends me, I am smart enough to hold my tongue about it, until I come across the thief myself.—J. of D., Vol. I., p. 255.

When I have gold and silver in my possession, which a thief may steal, or friends borrow, and never pay me back again, or which may take the wings of the morning, and I behold it no more, I only possess the negative of the true riches.—J. of D., Vol. I., p. 266.

If this people will do as they are told, will live their religion, walk humbly before their God, and deal justly with each other, we will make you one promise, in the name of Israel's God, that you will never be driven from the mountains.—J. of D., Vol. I., p. 319,

It is folly in the extreme for persons to say that they love God, when they do not love their brethren.—J. of D., Vol. I., p. 297.

Speaking as the world view men and things, in the eyes of the vast majority of mankind, the devil is the greatest gentleman that ever made his appearance on this earth.—J. of D., Vol. IV., p. 347.

I hope as I grow old, to grow wise. As I advance in years, I hope to advance in the true knowledge of God and godliness. I hope to increase in the power of the Almighty, and in influence to establish peace and righteousness upon the earth, and to bring all the sons and daughters of Adam and Eve, even all who will hearken to the principles of righteousness, to a true sense of the knowledge of God and godliness, of themselves, and the relation they sustain to heaven and heavenly beings.—J. of D., Vol. IV., p. 326.

It would be better if you and I never should have anything pertaining to this world, than to lose the spirit of the gospel and love the world.—J. of D., Vol. IV., p. 342.

The difficulty with the whole world in their divisions and subdivisions, is that they have no more confidence in each other than they have in their God, and that is none at all.—J. of D., Vol. IV., p. 296.

There never was that necessity; there never has been a time on the face of the earth, from the time that the church went to destruction, and the Priesthood was taked from the earth, that the powers of darkness and the powers of earth and hell were so embittered, and enraged, and incensed against God and godliness on the earth, as they are at the present. And when the spirit of persecution, the spirit of hatred, of wrath, and malice ceases in the world against this people, it will be the time that this people have apostatized and joined hands with the wicked, and never until then.—J. of D., Vol. IV., p. 327.

www.ingramcontent.com/pod-product-compliance
Lightning Source LLC
Chambersburg PA
CBHW020952030726
47496CB00005B/1468